CASSANDRA
MISREADS THE
BOOK of SAMUEL

& OTHER UNTOLD TALES OF THE PROPHETS

GIDON ROTHSTEIN

Preface and Acknowledgements

R. Shlomo Carlebach noted that a person can observe the Sabbath for the first time only once. Similarly, the stories of Scripture all too often are lost in the haze of familiarity that comes from having heard them before. It is my hope, with this collection, to place those same stories—some more familiar, some less—into new enough contexts that we will be able to see them again with the eyes of the first-time reader.

We all know the story of the Golden Calf, or at least we think we do until we watch people fairly similar to ourselves live through the event. Many of us know of Samuel the prophet, his anointing of Saul, his guiding of David through his entry into the kingship—but how would our perspective of him change if we were Cassandra, failed prophetess of Troy, and how would her insights into his life shape our own?

Success and failure are also themes not always considered when thinking about the lives of the prophets. How would Hosea have fared in trying to find a literary agent (a theme, obviously, somewhat close to my own heart)? Would Obadiah have looked back on his career with satisfaction or regret, and which emotion would have been more appropriate? What would it have been like for Haggai, Zachariah, and Malachi to strive for prophecy in an era in which it was clearly coming to an end?

These themes and more are touched in the storybook you hold in your hand. It is my hope that in reading them you—whatever your age, gender, or other affiliation—will find yourself drawn back into the world of Scripture, to reconsider again the project of prophecy and its legacy. As always, I hope you will share with me your thoughts on how well I have fulfilled this goal, at grothst@gmail.com.

In any writing, it is hard to separate whom to acknowledge for this instance of publishing and whom to thank for their general contributions to my life. In a book built off of Scripture, it would be particularly noticeable if I failed to express my gratitude to my Creator for having allowed me to contribute in this small way towards making His Word better known in the world—in addition to the too many other blessings I benefit from daily. As Scripture says, to Him, silence is the greatest praise.

My wife Elizabeth and our children, Tamar, Aryeh, and Adin, continue to provide support, pleasure, fun, and solace, all necessary pieces of a writer's life. My mother, my in-laws, and other family members—who are, I am happy to say, too numerous to mention by name—do so as well, and I thank each for all they do for me. The same applies to the various friends, readers, and critics who have enriched me personally and helped improve my writing.

The stories here had their germ in exercises assigned in a Gotham Writers' Workshop headed by Owen King, and I thank him for the spark that set me on this path. As with my previous book, *Murderer in the Mikdash*, the staff at Booksurge (John Rieck, Lindsay Parker, and others involved at particular stages of the process) has been unfailingly polite, upbeat, encouraging, and helpful.

Although they have no stake in my doing so, I wish to close with a word of thanks to all the prophets, not only those whose stories I have adapted here. Part of the preparation for this work was realizing the challenges they met in what might seem a simple task, getting God's Word heard and heeded. As I dedicate this book to their memory, it is with the hope that I may also contribute to that same goal.

pg 9, 101, 133

TABLE OF C

You Can't Change Human Nature

Experts claimed family dinners brought everyone closer. *They* said all the fighting and commotion would pay off in the unbreakable fellowship forged among those who had shared that table. That mantra guided Rock, how he and Penny got themselves through the nights when the kids were shouting, name-calling, and complaining as the family engaged in what passed for an evening meal.

On The Night, it started innocently enough. The younger ones were riled up, their mother trying to keep some calm. If they didn't get to sleep early, they would either not wake up in time for the festivities or be in beasts of a mood all day.

Little Rock said, "Did you see when he threw the gold and jewelry into the fire, Ma, did you?"

Penny's correction was automatic, the kind she gave a dozen times a week. "Not 'he,' dear, call people by their names and titles; it's more polite."

"All right," he conceded, "did you see when Aaron, our prophet from Egypt, threw the gold and jewelry into the fire, did you?"

She patted his head with the toothy smile that had been the first of her assets to captivate her husband. "Yes, dear, wasn't it exciting!? Kory, did *you* see when the Calf came out?"

Their youngest was eight and everyone's favorite, but they were never sure how much of the world he noticed.

"I did, but I couldn't figure out how he did it. I made fires all afternoon, threw things in, and nothing ever came out!"

Ordinarily, Rock would have handled this kind of question, but he was busy trying to draw out Jessica, the thirteen-year-old. The past eighty-nine days had been a trial; she was miserable at being forced to leave the only home she had ever known and doing her best to share that mood with all around her. In her direction, Rock said, "You look upset, or should I say, more upset than usual; did something new happen?"

Her face could not have drooped further if her favorite pet had died. "Mom took every *single* piece of gold I owned, even the ones I got from Britney, remember from across the street back in Goshen? *Mom* didn't give everything *she* has, so why should I have had to?" Three vipers would have been hard-pressed to replicate the venom in the girl's face and voice.

Penny jumped in, as she often did when he was about to make a concession to his only daughter. "You have some nerve complaining about me! I gave a lot more of my gold than you did, at least five stones' weight, and you're pointing fingers! How dare you! And besides, who do *you* need to wear jewelry for anyway, at your age! When you need to attract a man—"

Rock looked to where his in-laws sat, his face asking them to step in between the two; the women of the clan were, after all, from their side. When they shook their heads, amused at his trouble, he sighed, looked at his wife, and asked, "You donated your gold and jewelry?"

The answer came tripping off her lips, ignoring the censure in his tone. "Sure, they came around for donations, said it was this huge joint project. Said Aaron himself–"

Little Rock wasn't one to let his mother's mistake slide. "I thought you said names *and* titles, Ma! Oh, and could you pass more manna, please?"

As he had when she had corrected him, Penny absorbed the interruption without missing a beat. "They said that Aaron, our temporary leader, needed it for an important project. And here's a little more, Junior, but that's it, you've had your full share! Anyway, then when I saw what he had made, well, it took my breath away. To imagine that I had a share in producing our new leader! I can't wait for tomorrow."

Penny's parents clucked, a sound the family knew well and tended to ignore. People like them could never understand the kinds of compromises life required of those who didn't hide in the cocoon the Levitical clan constructed for themselves. Rock would never tell the kids, but it had been quite the challenge getting even their mother to understand the choices he had to make all the time. Reeducating one Levite to tolerate his lifestyle was as far as he was going; someone else could try with his in-laws.

The Teen chose then to burst in to the tent, oblivious to his lateness, his excited chatter elbowing aside all other conversation. In another of the tragic patterns of the boy's life, his news managed to rouse his grandfather to respond, the older man's brow darkening, a hint of storm threatening to break.

"Wait, what? You're part of the ceremony tomorrow?"

The Teen beamed in response. "I know, can you believe it? They had a dance-off, and at first I was just fooling around. But then I said to myself, *Hey, for someone who studied with the best teachers in all of Egypt, losing would be way too embarrassing,* and I got grooving. And now, what do you know, I'm center stage tomorrow!"

His siblings' whoops of excitement forestalled any more sober response. Instead, Penny shooed them all to bed, reminding them that they could not get out extra early unless they got a full night's rest. Each child came over to collect a kiss, hug, and smile from Rock, and then trooped off to his or her section of the tent.

Penny's parents used the younger children's exit as cover for their own. Kissing her grandson goodnight, Penny's mother broke routine by holding The Teen in an unusually long hug, then moving him to arm's length. Deep emotion or urgent speech was rare for her, so the whole tent stopped to watch as she looked deep into his eyes and said, "Please be careful! Remember what we were taught at the Mount!"

He hugged her again, laughed, and said, "What's the worst that could happen, Grandma, I'll pull a hamstring?"

Penny's father opened his mouth, but his wife placed a hand on his arm. Still, as the two of them walked out and passed Rock, he paused, throwing parting words over his shoulder, "Take care of your family, son; these are dangerous times."

With Penny tucking in the various children and doing her final cleaning for the night, only father and son were left at the table. Rock began, fighting to keep his rising temper out of his voice. "You didn't you think you should check about joining the ceremony?"

The Teen snorted. "If I were twelve! Has the fact of my fifteenth birthday slipped your memory?"

Rock continued, knowing he was about to reap a tantrum, keeping his voice calm in the face of it. "Because maybe your mother and I don't approve."

The Teen tensed, opened his mouth to speak, then shut it, pushed back from the table, and got up to mutter his way around the tent. Many of their conversations had pauses like this, so Rock sat, waiting for the next chapter.

Penny, back to clean off the table, spoke in a tone low enough that only her husband could hear, "Don't bring *me* into this. *I* didn't say I don't approve. I think it's great he's finally finding some worthwhile use for all that time he wasted with dancing. I always thought he was just doing it to avoid helping you bake the bricks. Who knew my boy would be front and center at a national ceremony?"

She wiped away a tear, all too aware of her husband's discomfort with her emotions. Back in Egypt, he hadn't had the time or patience to retreat in the face of crying, but now it had proven remarkably effective.

Rock looked from wife to son. He could tell Penny what her father had said, but she had long ago rejected his view of the world. For which Rock ought to thank God, since the old man must have warned her away from marrying him. A woman who looked like she did could have had any number of men from her own tribe, free of the taint of slavery. Besides, the comment had been made to him, not her.

But he had to say *something*; she had once given him the silent treatment for two weeks because he withdrew in the middle of an argument. If only to avoid that, he said, "You think it's great, do you? And the rules we all heard, what, forty days ago?"

The Teen popped back in before his mother had a chance. "Dad, you're so behind the times; that was then, the Calf is now. Get with the program, man!"

Penny hushed them, her hands reminding them that the children had only recently gotten to bed. Until there was audible snoring from the other side of the tent, anything said would be heard by the little pitchers lying on their deerskins.

The break gave Rock a chance to recite Grace and avoid continuing what he knew would turn even uglier. He stepped out into the shadows cast by the pillar of fire at the edge of the camp. Four other men were already there, chatting by the firelight. One, Roy, called out, "Things rough at home tonight, eh, Rock?"

He laughed, relieved to have found some community. "You know it. The way they're carrying on about the Calf and the festivities tomorrow—"

The others nodded, and Roy said, "Right. When I told them they had to wake up early so I could help slaughter the animals, the wife was furious. She kept yammering about how it was bad enough all her friends pressured her into giving up her best jewelry, now I was going to roust her out of bed at who knows what hour. Course, I wasn't going to take that kind of garbage, so I put her in her place."

Eli, a recent addition to the neighborhood, guffawed. "Yeah, I bet you put her in her place. Except that *she's* in her bed, and you're standing out here, pretending to be master of your household, waiting for everyone to fall asleep."

The laughter around the circle rang with the edge of nervousness, the uncertainty that hounded them all as they felt their way through the loss of power that came with the Exodus. When they had been working eighteen-hour days, they'd had a kind of dominance, their wives and children fully aware of how beholden they were to their breadwinner. It hadn't hurt that the women's desperation to have more children put them in a perpetually forgiving mood.

The wives' almost overnight change from loyal childbearers into homebodies, from temptresses rushing out to lure their husbands into impregnating them into staid family women, concerned more with their children and the women's projects around the camp than with pleasing their husbands, weighed on all the men around that fire, indeed, around the camp.

Rock chewed the fat with the boys until he was sure he could have peace and quiet when he went back inside. He pulled back the flap, cursing when the swath of light it let in shined right on The Teen, who woke up.

"Dad, is that you?"

"Yeah, go back to bed."

"No, wait, I want to talk about this. It bugs me that you can't be happy for me; this is a really big deal. If I get to dance at these ceremonies, I might be promoted for the next festival, and from there, well, who knows?"

Rock bought time by taking a breath deep enough to fill his lungs, looking to pick words that had a chance of resonating with his firstborn. "Son, I *am* happy you're succeeding, and that you're excited. But did you think when I was slaving away, taking blows from the taskmasters so other Hebrews would stay out of trouble, that I did that for something like…this? Did you think that was how you honored me, by choosing Egyptian ways? When you tried out for the festivities, you made a choice, a choice for our past ways of worshiping God. You don't want me to criticize it, fine, I won't, but I can't pretend it thrills me."

The Teen turned over, muttering inaudibly. Rock considered forcing him to speak up, but decided against it. It would be bad enough tomorrow; no need to get into it tonight.

A few hours later, in tents across the camp, husbands woke up, hustling to get the manna before it melted in the morning sun. True, there would be meat at the ceremonies, but there was dinner to worry about. In his tent, Rock groaned and blinked his eyes open, not yet remembering why the harridan was shaking him so early. Groaning again, he moved to The Teen, knowing it would take more effort than Penny had had to expend getting him up.

The boy bolted upright at his father's first touch, not awake but ready to lash out at whoever had disturbed him. "What? What do you want?" Then, as consciousness worked its way over his horizon, "What time is it? It's still way dark outside; what're you, nuts?"

Rock knew only the truth, one of his main weaknesses. "Your mother says we have to get the food; she wants at least the little kids to have had breakfast, in case it runs long."

The Teen had already lain back down and pulled a blanket over his head. "Please, Pop, can't someone else go with you today? I've gotta be well rested for the rituals—you don't know what it's like, how much energy I'm going to be using. Just let me have another hour, 'til you come back with the food, pleeeeeeaaaaaase?"

Rock sighed. "Come on, you know it doesn't work that way. You're an adult now, and if you don't go yourself, there won't be any for you. And if your mother sees you skipping breakfast, she's going to give *me* hell, so get yourself up."

"Can't one of the kids go?"

"They're still sleeping. Not to mention underage." The Teen was out of bed, but the grumbling would continue until Rock put a stop to it. "And, by the way, if you wake one or all of them, you'll have yourself a companion for the entire day."

The threat hit the mark, quieting him down. Rock tried not to listen, knowing there would be no way to win.

The boy didn't speak again until they were at the edge of the camp, looking for where the food had rained down. He huffed along, head down, keeping up only when his father either prodded him or came to a complete stop to wait for him. Then he'd jog a few steps, but slow down as soon as his father continued walking.

When they reached the dewy spread of daily victuals, Rock looked back at the camp. The first lights of dawn were breaking the black of the horizon, the pillar of fire at camp's edge beginning its transformation into cloud. The group that gathered daily to witness the change was less than half its usual size.

Rock turned, surprised the Calf had stolen so many of the Transformation Watchers, to find The Teen grinning. Lifting his manna-filled hands in his father's direction, he said, "I got mine, Pop. Where's yours? Slowing down in your old age?"

He bent down to take food, the effort being literally more important than how much he actually picked up. Ticking off family members in his head, he bent three times for himself, three for Penny, three for Jessica, three for Little Rock, and three for Kory. That should be enough to get a day's food for each, he thought.

His stomach growled with the memory of the days he had come home without having worked hard enough at the food collection to please the-powers-that-be, to find only four portions in his pile. Penny was clear about who suffered for such mishaps; it took an extraordinarily good mood on those days for her to give him any food at all.

Done, he stepped toward his waiting son, hoping the teasing signaled an opening for a conversation. As they made their way back, he said, "I'm sorry about last night. I love you, and I want what's best for you."

"You've got a funny way of showing it."

This was an old and familiar issue between them. "Sure, I know you want me to jump into these new movements with more enthusiasm, that my wait-and-see attitude drives you crazy. But if you'd listen to me a little more, you'd realize that things aren't as simple as you think."

They suspended the conversation as they reached the tent, knowing better than to violate Penny's warning about bickering. She had the kids up and dressed, anxious to get to the center of camp before they missed anything.

At the sight of the food, she started in on her husband. "Come on, come on, give it to me already. I've got to fry it for your princess daughter, singe it for Little Rock, and scramble it for Kory. Where's the kindling?"

The faces of father and son told her the answer. She clucked her tongue in disgust, fussing the manna into portions and putting away the rest for the evening meal. "Is it too much to ask? Once a day, that's it, once a day, they have to go out and get their food—and that's God's choice, not mine. And then a little bit of firewood, so we don't have to swallow it cold." Looking up to Heaven, a gesture the family knew too well, she finished, "Is that too much, Lord? Tell me, am I asking too much?"

Rock took his portion in silence and went to the corner of the tent that best shielded him from her. Closing his eyes, he brought to mind a morning cake he had once seen the Royal Baker himself prepare. Thinking hard, he bit in, delighted at the taste of honey dribbling down his throat, an almost perfect replica of the fluffy bread-cake.

Kory was too young to understand the protocols of his mother's moods and tried to help her free herself of her anger. "C'mon, Ma, cheer up. I love my manna cold; usually I save it for Sabbath mornings, but it'll be a nice change of pace. Today, I want it to taste of wine and oil mixed into the flour itself." Scrunching his face together for concentration, he took a bite. "Ummmmmmmmmm! So don't worry, Ma, we're fine."

She turned her fury on him. "Good, is it? And these last three weeks, me slaving over the fire to ready it, what was that, an empty gesture? You've got such a powerful imagination, from now on, *you* make it in the morning!"

Their parents' sullen retreat to neutral corners of the tent had come an hour earlier than usual, leaving the kids to breakfast together. They ate in silence, occasionally wondering aloud what the rest of the day would be like.

Jessica would have suggested taking the boys herself, but her tongue still stung from the lashing it had taken the last time she had let the neighbors catch a hint of family discord. Instead, she checked and rechecked the two boys, then stood them at the door, reminding them to be silent so the parents would have no excuse to say, "That's it, we're not going."

Rock and Penny knew they had to seem happy when they stepped outside the tent, or spark even more gossip. Tossing their fury on the heap of unresolved arguments that came close to smothering the love buried underneath, they dragged out their best smiles as they held hands to walk in public. The dawn had broken even if the sun was not yet up, and streams of people were making their way to the center of the camp.

The excited chatter, the attempts to figure out what would come next, was reminiscent of the Exodus itself. "Did you hear about the games?" "Who do you think will win the competitions?" "I can't wait for the roasted sacrifices!"

At this last, Rock turned to his wife. The children knew that look, tensed to see whether it was humor or bile. "I guess *we'll* be too full from breakfast to eat any roast sacrifice, huh?"

The Teen couldn't miss a chance. "Not me, Pop. I left my portion for later."

The boy's underdeveloped sense of humor came from Penny directly, so she knew he had missed his father's point. She said, "He wasn't serious, Misha. You know we're not eating from any sacrifice."

The boy's whine managed to mix horror with awareness that he could not win this fight. "What do you meeeean? I *told* all my friends I'd meet them. I'm signed up for like seven of the games, besides the dancing, and my coach thinks I'm a lock to medal in Place a Bowl of Fruit before the Calf. But I need holy meat in my system to do my best!"

She tried again, softening a little in the face of his distress. "C'mon, Misha, your father and I have always been clear that that is not our way. The dancing was one thing, but you should have known we wouldn't be eating. The games either, for that matter..."

The other children knew to avoid confrontation, were already expert in circumventing their parents when needed. The Teen stepped into the fight rather than away. "No, of course not. But you're going to go and enjoy, am I right? You're such hypocrites; you *know* worshiping the Calf is right, and you sit back and let others be the leaders! You make me sick."

Rock started to explain, but the first call for the dancers came from the center. The Teen mumbled something that might have been "I don't want to be late" and ran off.

The crowds posed a problem for the policemen trying to maintain a clear area around the Calf. To help, members of the tribes on each side of the center of the camp were constructing a human cordon about fifty cubits from the Calf itself. Rock joined a group helping build a platform for better viewing.

They finished just as the call for silence rippled outward from the center. Looking around, Rock asked the guy next to him, "Where's Aaron?"

He shrugged in response, as did the next five people. Rock relayed the information to Penny, his heart lifting at the confusion on her face. When she asked how he could miss such an occasion, he almost kissed her. Moments like these, where they saw the world as no one around them seemed to, reminded him why he had married her.

He put Kory on his shoulders but forgot to preemptively calm Little Rock. "Daaaaaad! How come Kory gets to go on your shoulders and not me? It's not faaaaaaair!"

There was no way to salvage the situation now, Rock knew, and no way to avoid this interchange. "You'll get a turn in a few minutes."

Little Rock folded his arms, stamped his feet, and frowned. "No, it's not fair! He's always getting the first turn! You love him better! Everyone loves him better!"

He turned to storm off, as he had seen his older brother do so often, but Rock put a hand on his shoulder. "I'm sorry you're upset, but you can't go wandering."

"I don't want to stand with you!"

"Again, I'm sorry you're mad, and your mother and I would love it if you would stay here. We would enjoy it more, and we think you would, too. But if you refuse," Rock said this last with hand upraised to stop the protests about to spew forth, "you can stand anywhere between here and over there," he waved at an area ten cubits away, "where your mother and I can see you."

Little Rock chose the farthest allowed spot, frown still firm and prominent in each of his facial features. A wave of quiet spread over the crowd from the middle as the master of ceremonies' voice boomed, almost as loud as the One on Sinai forty days before. "Ladies and Gentlemen, welcome to this morning's celebration! It is with pride and quite a bit of excitement that we present, for the first time, the God Who Took Us Out of Egypt!"

The power of his vocal cords was remarkable, carrying through the assemblage without the kind of amplification Moses had at the Mount or having others repeat his words. The silence gave way to a cheer as he finished.

And then the sacrifices began. Rock's children competed over how many different slaughterings they could watch up close, racing back and forth to their father, who had been pressed into service as scorekeeper. Soon enough, the killing turned to skinning and roasting, the heat of the numerous fires sweeping away any remaining morning chill.

Once the last goat had been killed, the three rejoined their parents, babbling stories of mortally wounded sheep breaking away from their former owners, blood splattering throughout the camp as the crowd bludgeoned the fleetest animals to death.

Penny worked her way further into her husband's heart by heading off any pleadings to eat sacrificial meat. Pulling manna out of her bag, she handed each of the children a piece and regaled them with memories of taste, texture, and happy occasions when they had eaten other meat. The boys listened, eyes closed, focused on getting the memories in their heads into the food in their mouths.

Speaking while chewing, Kory looked to his dad. "But I don't understand. If we're not going to join everyone else in worship, why come?"

There was no good way to explain it to an eight-year-old. "Do you remember, before we left Egypt, how hard I used to work?"

The boy nodded, tears welling in his eyes. "And do you remember how I sometimes looked when I got home?"

The puppy eyes on his son tugged at Rock's heart, but the lesson needed to be taught. "I remember, Daddy. I used to cry when I saw how those men beat you."

He hugged the boy and gave him a quick kiss on the cheek before standing up again. "Then maybe you can understand why your mother and I agreed that my days of getting involved were over. The risk, the pain—it wasn't worth it."

The cries from the crowd rose a notch as the selected dancers arranged themselves in rows. The young bodies, not yet ravaged by time or childbearing, gyrated in a synchronized and hypnotizing rhythm. The adults stared, mouths slack, breath moving in and out of their lungs only enough to avoid asphyxiation, their yearning to be chosen for holy sex written on their faces and in their postures.

For Rock, it was a tawny-haired girl four rows back. Not that he would agree if she approached him, he assured himself, but the chance to say no to a girl like that would be worth...well, anyway, the wife would appreciate him more once she saw the opportunity he had turned down for her.

His ruminations were interrupted by a tug on his sleeve. "Dad, you didn't finish. What do you mean it wasn't worth it?"

He hushed the boy, not wanting to miss the moment the girl caught his eye. Then, embarrassed at how entranced he'd gotten, he bent down, giving his son one more hug.

Squatting, he answered, "It wasn't worth it because there's no real right and wrong; it's what whoever's leading decides. And then they punish whoever was competing with them. Your mother and I decided not to play that game anymore. Others can do what they want, but our family says our thoughts and choices stay in our tent. We don't criticize others, and we want the same in return. And that's it."

Jessica broke the contemplative silence that had hovered between her brother and father. "Look, look, there he is!"

Penny said, "Who? Who? Where?"

Following the line of her finger, they saw The Teen. He had finished some series of moves they couldn't see from their angle, but the whooping cheers from nearby said he had done them well. Now he was wading into the stands to select his partner for the next phase. Without hesitation, as if he had known whom he would take, he grabbed the hand of a woman from the tribe over, a beauty fifteen years his elder.

Ignoring her husband's protests, he led her back into the middle, where they intertwined and excited each other so quickly that the leaders moved them right next to the Calf for greater visibility. As those who were running the ceremonies had hoped, The Teen and his paramour's cries inspired imitation, people pairing off almost at random throughout the camp to serve the Calf with their mating.

Rock could feel the red rising to his face. It was bad enough the boy didn't listen within their home, but to so publicly violate family values was too much. He moved to push his way through, but Penny stopped him.

"They'll tear you apart." And she spread her arms right and left, the transfixed multitudes in heat confirming her claim.

He yielded to her greater wisdom. Besides, they had their hands full trying to distract the children from realizing how this Calf was worshiped. Luckily, the Levites arrived, more than enough to catch the kids' attention. Kory saw his grandfather first and shouted, pointing, "Look, Dad, there's Grandpa, with that whole group of Leviim. What are they doing?"

Rock followed the boy's finger, saw them moving through the camp, saying their piece, taking notes, and continuing on, never raising their voices, never fighting. As they approached, he could hear snippets of words, the whole becoming audible only when they were almost on him. His father-in-law's voice was the most distinct, at least for Rock, who had had to listen to it for years. "Go back to your tents! They would never do this if they didn't have an audience! Walk away; it will end here, and we can still avoid the Lord's wrath!"

They made no visible impact but kept on, indefatigable in their search for even one who would hear them and step back from the precipice of sin. Rock turned to Penny. "Perhaps we should listen to your father," and then added, to help her with the difficult task of admitting the previous generation had gotten something right, "if only to keep the young ones from seeing what they shouldn't."

She hesitated. "But think of the neighbors; I can hear them now. 'Did you see who thought they were too good for Calf-worship? Look who's holier-than-thou!' It's bad enough we didn't eat, but if we leave now, we'll be the talk of the neighborhood. It can't be that much longer anyway."

They stayed, which had the advantage of allowing them to watch events unfold, so that in future years they did not have to wonder whether they might have changed the outcome. The Levites' determination never flagged, their strategy changing only when they came upon those engaged in active Calf-worship. To *them*, they would say, "Be warned, Children of Israel. What you now do is idol-worship, prohibited by God, punishable by death."

The targets of these warnings laughed, renewed their efforts without responding, or said, "Got it, thanks." Stopping was out of the question, a waste of too good an opportunity to revel in the freedom the Calf had bestowed.

When the Levites reached The Teen, two of them administered the warning. He looked up, paused long enough to say, "Oh, hi, Grandpa, enjoying the day?" Then, turning to the two, he said, "Yes, I heard you, but I think I'll keep going, thanks." And he rejoined his partner in their effort to win the prize for loudest coupling.

Rock again took a step in their direction. Penny pulled him back. "Tempting, isn't it? Makes you long a bit for your days in enforcement?"

He smiled. "Am I that transparent?"

She returned his look and shrugged her shoulders. "Once a cop, always a cop; I knew that when I married you. But," she anticipated him, "you promised those days

26

were done. It was one of the reasons I agreed to marry a slave, remember?"

He sputtered. "But look at this—"

She shook her head. "Irrelevant; they're not hurting anyone, they're doing what they think is right, and it's none of our business. That was our agreement, no?"

Rock hung his head at the reminder. It had been like tearing out a piece of himself, and today's events had ripped off the scab. He knew she was right, that live-and-let-live was the only way to build a nation as diverse as this one. Knowing it didn't make it any easier on his gut, which longed for action.

The next few minutes challenged Penny in other ways, since she had to fend off invitations from boys no older than The Teen, and to save Jessica from those who thought of initiating her. Rock spent the time holding his breath, praying all this would end before their lack of participation would draw attention.

The sound of stones smashing answered his prayers. Moses stood at the edge of the camp, the dust of the smashed Tablets swirling around his face as if it had come from his nose or ears, his height making him visible to all. The fury in his eyes squelched any thoughts people may have had about getting back to their activities.

He moved to the center, the crowd melting to open a path. Striding up to the Calf, he paused only long enough to shake his head at the enormity of the crime, then took all the surrounding torches to make a bonfire under it. Once it had melted, he smashed the metal to bits, dissolved it in water, and called people over, forcing them to drink.

Rock turned to Penny, the urgency in his voice the same as when they had almost gotten caught outside during the hailstorm. "We've got to get out of here."

27

She furrowed her brows. "Why?"

He shook his head. "No time. Get the kids."

The call, "Who is for God to me!" stopped him. He was for God, wasn't he? He turned to Penny, "Maybe I should…"

She laughed at him. "You tell me to get the kids, but I think I need to get *you*, keep *you* out of trouble. Come on, mister, we're outta here!"

They ran home, their progress blocked by Levites, swords out, guiding traffic. At the checkpoint, each family was stopped while the troops examined them. Most often, the Levites looked, shook their heads no, and the people passed. Once, though, two of them looked at a man, then said, one after the other, "That's him; we saw him."

Faster than Rock could have guessed, they convened a court. The two witnesses testified to having warned the man, the judges briefly cross-examined them, and then executed their judgment. Rock covered Kory's eyes with one hand, Little Rock's with the other, relieved that Penny had been quick enough to do the same for Jessica. No one gasped or protested, as if this were not the first summary execution they had seen. The line moved forward, Rock hoping all the people in front of him were innocent. At least the kids wouldn't have to go through that again.

All the way home—as they waited in line, as they tried not to look guilty while the Levites examined them, as they commiserated with others after they had made it through, as they complained about the excesses of the self-appointed security services—a thought niggled at Rock, some piece of unfinished business. It wasn't until they got to the tent that it broke through into his consciousness. "Wait, we only took the little ones!"

Penny's face whitened, eyes widening in a look he had not seen since the last time he took a particularly bad beating from the taskmasters. "You've got to find him!"

He ran out, heading again toward the middle of the camp, pausing at each checkpoint to ask if anyone had seen The Teen. When he got to where he had been standing during the ceremonies, he saw a huge line snaking to where the Calf itself had been. Security was tighter, Levites manning the sides and back as well as the front. Rock recognized several of The Teen's friends, who had been performing near him that morning.

Casting his eyes forward, his spirits rose a little when he did not see his son. Better, the judge at the front was, thank God, Penny's father. His first thought at the sight of the old man, upraised sword in hand, ready to execute a verdict, was that at least this was not where The Teen would be punished.

His relief was short-lived as his eyes caught sight of the previous defendant. It was the woman who had been The Teen's partner, her corpse still actively bleeding. Heart sinking, Rock looked back at his father-in-law, this time focusing on the defendant held in a kneeling position before him. The Levites were finishing their testimony. Their words were inaudible from that distance, but the sword began its swift journey down.

Before the nightmare became a reality, before he was thrown into the mourning that would never fully recede, Rock had time for a last bitter thought. *The experts claimed family meals brought everyone closer together. The experts didn't know squat.*

29

BOOK OF SAMUEL, CHAPTERS 1–3

Visions in her sleep were a new torment, so new Cassandra did not realize it had been a dream when she first heard the words, "Speak, Lord, for your servant is listening." She bolted up, scanning her room for who had spoken.

Starting at the door opposite her bed, she cast her eyes left, over the clothes chest, the pots and jugs on their shelves, ending at the small statue of Athena that protected her in the night. Calming a little as the first half of her search failed to reveal an intruder, she repeated the exercise on the other side, from the chair in the corner to the table covered with books. She relaxed only when she arrived at the candle that ensured she would never be in complete darkness.

Her heart returning to normal, she lay back down and closed her eyes. Leftover images floated in her head, and she followed them with the drowsy half interest she assumed would fade into sleep.

Only it didn't, keeping her awake with an insistence she knew well from the daytime. After waiting several more long moments, sleep hovering out of reach, she heaved her the-gods-*again!?* sigh, took the candle to the table, and picked up the stylus and a tablet. Recording it permanently was the only sure way to free her mind of it, which might mean she could get back to sleep.

Start with the characters; they always want you to focus on people, she warned herself. There had been Hannah, hair so black it lightened her dark skin, proud nose jutting only slightly less far than the ripe breasts made for nursing. A pleasing-looking woman, her attractiveness fouled only by the sour downturn of her mouth. The flat stomach told of her barrenness, a shame that more than explained her bitter set of face. Cassandra winced as she wrote, glancing down at her own tapered middle.

She jotted the outline she could expand later when dictating to the scribe, thankful the pieces of the dream came back slowly enough to accommodate her ineptness with the writing tool. The second wife, Peninah, looked nice enough—plump body, smiling face—but Hannah recoiled when she entered the room.

The barbs the heavier woman let fly as soon as she walked in justified the reaction, piercing Cassandra as much as the woman in her dream.

Peninah said, "What do you contribute? At least my children are out there in the fields, helping our husband sow and reap! *I've* given him posterity, not to mention sources of support for our older years. How much longer do you think he will keep a useless woman around to consume his harvests?"

She responded with the meekness of failures everywhere. "Please, allow me my wretchedness in peace. Granted you are right, what can I do?"

Victory was not enough, although Peninah's persistence puzzled Cassandra. It was not meanness that drove her, but a sense of mission, the nature of which eluded Cassandra. "Do? Surely *I* don't know. I would think *you* could figure out why the Lord denies you fruit of the womb. The answer lies in yourself, not in your stars. Do *something*, and perhaps the Good Lord will give you what you seek!"

It came back in pieces, not fully fleshed out, tantalizing the Trojan woman with its implication of a message she was supposed to decipher. She wrote, waiting for catharsis, the feeling of *there, that's what it's telling me*, but it did not come. Worse, the memories also refused to fade and let her get on with her life.

She watched as Hannah moped at family meals, shared her jealousy at Elkanah's obvious enjoyment of the excited and talkative children ranged on either side of his table. He would often turn his salt-and-pepper beard to his childless wife, trying to involve her in the conversation. Peninah sat at the other end, beaming, soundlessly basking in her children's hold on their father's affections. As long as she had them, her face said, her hold on his heart was secure.

The stylus hovering above the tablet, Cassandra lost track of the dream, her own family overtaking her thoughts. Her siblings' children had invaded her father's house in much the same way, each cute toddler highlighting to all, especially Father, Cassandra's failures as a woman and as a daughter.

Try as he might, he would never convince her it didn't matter. He could take her to the public ceremonies, pay extra attention to her at family gatherings, but his pain was always just behind his eyes. No matter how much she went where he asked, smiled as if she were enjoying herself, she knew he'd never relax until she found a man and bore him children.

The dream-recall allowed personal musings for only so long. Elkanah reclaimed center stage, his pleas to Hannah to be comforted by his love falling on four deaf ears. *Men!* Cassandra spat in her thoughts. *Say what he wants, favorite wife or not, I bet anything he gets Peninah pregnant before returning to Hannah's bed.*

The drop of saltwater that fell from her eye and erased the last few words gave her only a moment's warning. Jumping away from the table, she turned the tablet over to protect it while trying to staunch the flow of tears with her other hand.

Too late. Disturbing as the dream itself was, the tragedy of its having come at night had finally registered with her subconscious, and the liquid flooded out of her eyes. *Why, Apollo, why? Marriage, children, friends, all this you took from me; you need to rob me of my sleep as well?*

By the time the crying ended, the Hebrew family had faded. Freed, she could fool herself into thinking it was a one-time aberration, arrange herself on the bearskin bed, and fall into a blessedly dreamless sleep.

She woke suddenly, the high sun telling her how late she was. Cursing, she rushed around her room, dressing. If she missed the gossip circle, they would each ask after her welfare, especially her mental health. The revenge she knew her mother would take for having to face that kind of questioning turned Cassandra's jog to the palace into a madcap dash.

Despite her persistent dithering over whether her daughter needed to be locked away, Hecuba remained the only person who stoked the embers of emotion in Cassandra's heart. The sixty-year-old's grace and carriage reflected the internal ease, the calm acceptance of life, that soothed all fortunate enough to have her shine it on them.

She was in the salon, the sewing group already hard at work spreading stories, the only real purpose of their gatherings Cassandra had ever been able to see. She waited outside the circle of women she had known since childhood—the kind of adopted relatives who can never

34

be escaped, but seem to always find new ways to make one regret having a family—looking for her mother's sign to enter.

When she was called forward, she moved through, kissing each woman she passed. Some flinched, afraid of what physical contact might spark. Most accepted, resigned to the price they had to pay for being part of the queen's inner circle.

Hecuba lifted her cheek to receive her daughter's kiss and patted her on the back, face and gesture conveying relief at her daughter's willingness to be seen in public. The others used the next ten minutes to discover reasons to leave, backing out of the room as from the presence of a serpent whose tongue can flick death at any moment.

Cassandra apologized, teasing, "I seem to have gotten in the way of catching up on the dalliances of the day."

The queen patted the sofa perpendicular to the one on which she reclined. "No matter, dear, the juiciest tidbits were dispensed long before you got here. Besides, it gives us some time in private. How are you? Headache? Throat raw? Bruises?"

The questions shocked Cassandra, confronting her with how fully the dream had pushed aside thoughts of the previous day's events. She was no less surprised at the answer, since a fit usually left her with each of the symptoms her mother had named.

Hecuba sighed. "For at least that kindness we can thank the gods. But as you said, the Destroyer has returned."

It was the name she had used in the throes of her episode. Of course she should have skipped the annual competitions, but, as so often, she had been unable to resist her father's invitation and importunings.

The oddsmakers, like the rest of Troy, had expected Hector to sweep the combats, Deiphobus the decathlon. Cassandra's older brother had done his part, defeating all challengers in both wrestling and swordplay, but an unknown shepherd from Mount Ida took seven of the ten track events. During the javelin throw, one of the upstart's incessant taunts went too far, and the favorite, in his fury, aimed his spear at his opponent instead of the far field.

A glimpse of Deiphobus' arm as it began to move forward brought the words from her throat. "O glad day, he kills the Destroyer! Paris will die, Priam's prodigal removed! The solution urged so long ago comes to fruition, here in the city itself! O glad day, he kills the Destroyer! Paris will die, Priam's prodigal removed! The solution urged so long ago comes to fruition, here in the city itself! O glad day—"

Deiphobus dropped his hand, like a child caught with a hand in the cookie jug. Registering the approval in her words, he raised it again, but too late. The people nearby tackled him, unwilling to let their city bear the centuries-long shame of having allowed the death of a competitor in a state-sponsored contest.

The immediate danger avoided, everyone froze, waiting for the king to guide them in how to react. Priam—king of Troy, father of Hector, Cassandra, and, at least if her vision could be believed, this nimble shepherd—led his retinue over to the unknown man, leaving his daughter to recover from her paroxysm.

After exchanging the formal and traditional greetings, "Ho, stranger, Ho, Majesty," the king shifted into his public voice. "On behalf of the city of Troy, on behalf of the contestants and spectators, let me congratulate you on races well run. You have earned your garland today, and we are all, indeed, privileged to have seen such a fine athlete in action. Tell us, young man, who are you, whence do you hail?"

The champion's voice evinced none of the strength of his arms and legs. Priam had been standing perhaps three arms' lengths away from the lad, yet had to lean forward to hear him. The others got his reply on a wave of repeat questions and answers, each person asking of the one in front, answering the one behind, alternating between "Whad'desay?" and "He said, 'They call me Paris, Majesty, as yonder woman declared, not the other names, neither Destroyer nor prodigal.'"

Hecuba's accepting her characterization of Paris was too overwhelming for Cassandra to absorb, so her question came out neutrally, almost casually, as if the answer were of no consequence. "What makes you think I was right in calling him Destroyer?"

The queen narrowed her eyes, a common enough occurrence when she had to speak candidly with the woman of hair-trigger nerves she called daughter. "Dear, how do you think it came about that Paris was not raised in the palace?"

"His nurse kidnapped him." It took saying it out loud as an adult to realize the flimsiness of the old family tale; it was hard to imagine even her childhood self had swallowed that. "Least, that's what you always told us."

"Yes, sweet one, we did. But the truth is…well, the truth is…I mean, the truth is…"

Cassandra resisted stamping her foot. "Yes, Mother, the truth is?"

Hecuba's eyes glistened. "Do you remember how angry your father was the day Paris was born, when we called for you and Hector?"

"I remember." They had been playing Walk-The-Wall, violating a taboo so strict she to this day would not dare admit it. Stashing the safety ropes had taken time, and they had entered the birthing chamber many minutes after the summons. "It was because we were late, I always assumed."

Her mother shook her head. "We let you think that because it was easier than the truth. Which was," she let out a breath, hanging on to each second before she had to make her revelation, "that I had had a vision."

Cassandra's heart beat a little faster. "I'm sorry, what?"

"Yes, dear, not dissimilar from your…incidents. I saw the baby's head ringed by a halo of fire, the city burning in the middle. When you and Hector arrived, your father and I were arguing about it. After the fever took Helenus, your father was desperate for another son. The thought of killing it—him—to prevent the vision from coming true did not sit well."

Cassandra's head spun, the mention of her dead twin the least of it. She shoved most of it aside for later; she needed to focus on the immediate concerns. "But then you know what he will do, what we must do! Why aren't you arguing with Father, getting him to act now, before it's too late?"

The imperial and imperious raise of Hecuba's hand told her daughter she had edged too close to a dangerous line. "Daughter, you seem to have forgotten our place. It took all of my strength the first time to get him to agree, and even then he did what he wanted. I've never seen him as happy as yesterday, when Paris was returned to him, as champion of the decathlon no less. We can only wait and watch the gods' plan unfold. They are the gods; they will do what is good in their eyes."

The words sent Cassandra back to a part of the dream she had not remembered earlier. She could nod as if listening, but her attention had been captured by the two men blessed with the good looks of those in the prime of life. Their tall backs were unbent by age or worry, their heads crowned with bountiful hair, the one straight, the other curly. Women of Troy would fall over each other for the chance to spend long nights running their hands through these manes.

Not that they needed Trojan women, the dream making a point of how adept they were at fending for themselves in that regard. The unmarried Hebrew women who came to make offerings were taken to their beds, the married ones offered that more delicious pleasure of flirting with the lines, both sides testing how far they could go without acting on it, seeing who could titillate the other more, break off when holding the upper hand of frustration.

The two men yielded their place in her mind to their father Eli, a man she figured for at least seventy-five, with failing eyesight. *Sure,* came the bitter gibe in her head, *men can wait until their forties or later to have children, but here I am, pretty much done at thirty-six.*

His stooped entry to his house was a lesson in the triumph of determination over the infirmities of a body well into its decline into death. Focused on the chair that would hold him until bedtime, he did not hear his sons enter, did not see their smirks as they nudged each other, pointing to his weakened condition.

Once he got settled, they greeted him loudly, leaning toward his right side, but ignored his response as they bustled about laying out dinner. He waited for them to notice him, but finally called them over, an interruption that instigated another round of filial eye-rolling.

"Father, you know we're hungry; can't this wait? You do remember getting up at dawn and working a whole day offering sacrifices, don't you?"

Eli's deafness, physical or purposeful, inured him to their protest. "My sons, I hear distressing word of the goings-on at the Sanctuary, despite our previous conversations. Do you know how disappointing I find this?"

A quick hand-sign negotiation left Hofni to respond. He crossed his arms and tapped his foot as he said, "Father, you have to understand that matters are different than when you were running the show. Without building up our volume of visitors, the Sanctuary might not have the funds to continue. So few even come, we need to squeeze as much out of each of them as we can. It's not our fault women are easier than men, and if we get some fringe benefits, well, no harm, no foul, you know?"

"Cassandra, are you listening?"

She had forgotten to keep nodding in time with her mother's story. "Sorry, my mind wandered."

"Another outburst?"

The sympathetic tone might have lured Cassandra into an honest answer. Only her fear of the physicians stayed her mouth; one wrong step and her mother might yield to their repeated pleadings to take her in for residential care. The thought, or threat, helped her relax her face, answer in her sanest voice.

"Not at all, my mind just wandered; I apologize. You were saying you did not think you could convince Father to get rid of him a second time?"

"No, *dear*, I was *saying* that Paris was clearly a member of this family, since he has already made clear that he is not willing to heed my words."

Cassandra patted her mother's arm, the dream offering a comforting response. "Don't fret, Mother; something tells me even fathers can have trouble bringing wayward sons into line."

The knowledge that Hecuba had believed one of her prophecies buoyed Cassandra. The good mood apparently kept the gods at bay, leaving her outburst- and dream-free for the first time in twenty years. Cautiously, she started rebuilding her life. She went to sleep early, woke well rested, and greeted people in the street, beginning to believe she would not be forced to scream the manner of their death at total strangers. She even looked up friends she'd had to drop when her "problem" first compelled a retreat from polite society.

She spent long hours in the queen's chambers, making sure her mother was fully aware of the improvement. She chatted with the gossip circle, laughed at their inanities, fluttered her hands, touched up her hair every few minutes, inquired after the latest fashions of clothing, makeup, and perfume. The weeks eased worry lines out of Hecuba's face as much as Cassandra's.

Paris ruined it, as she should have known he would. The morning of the beginning of the end, Cassandra had noticed her mother's distracted inattention but nattered on, happy to trade one impoliteness for years of her mother's overlooking her more serious infractions. After an hour or two of drivel interrupted only by pro forma questions from the queen, she decided to excuse herself before the gossips arrived.

"Well, Mother, it was nice to see you, but I told Atheneas we'd have lunch near the amphitheater…"

Hecuba stayed her daughter, waving for the retinue of attendants to indulge them with a moment alone. Once they left, she turned to face Cassandra head-on, sat herself up a little straighter, and said, "There is something I must tell you, and it will distress you, perhaps more than it does me."

Her mother's pause to fortify herself gave the rumbling in Cassandra's stomach, so silent these past weeks, a chance to return. "Paris has taken some ships, wouldn't tell us where he was going, how long he'd be gone. He said weeks, maybe four, maybe forty."

The backbeat in her brain, never fully silenced, kicked up a notch, and the rumbling turned into nausea. She had to fight the urge to flee before a fit embarrassed her, so she could ask the necessary questions.

"How many ships? Did he say why, when he only just came back?"

Hecuba tilted her head and scrunched one eye, a look of pain at how little she knew of Paris' intentions. "He said he thought he should tour Hellas, celebrate his reinstatement as...I think he wanted to say crown prince, but was afraid Hector would hear."

She paused, eyes looking at a point beyond the wall, struggling with how to continue. "I tell you, dear, the two of them are a puzzle. Hector is older, stronger, has lived in Troy all his life, is obviously a better candidate for when your father...when time marches on. But Paris, in just the few weeks he's been home, somehow seems to always manipulate people in the direction that suits him. He is more of a survivor than your older brother, and I suspect he will gain more prominence in the annals as well."

The match between her mother's analysis and what the gods had told her would at other times have cheered Cassandra. The more she could think she was like her mother, the more she could hold on to the wild hope that her outbursts might one day settle into something more tolerable. Right now, she could not indulge that fantasy.

"Mother, why didn't you stop him? No good can come of this, I am sure."

The queen reached out to stroke her daughter's hair. "You're right, but there's nothing for us to do. We can only wait and watch what the gods send our way."

The returning dream was going to distract her too much to be able to even pretend to carry on a conversation. Feigning to be crushed by the news about Paris, she excused herself with the urgency her mother knew so well.

Now it was Eli at dinner, sons nowhere to be seen, turning his head at the loud knocking on the door, calling for the visitor to enter. The lines on the face of the man who entered, and the gray in his hair, were at odds with his physical youthfulness.

He, too, Cassandra could tell, had been required to deliver upsetting revelations for many years. Striding up to the aged priest, he announced himself as a man of God, told of the god's anger at the misuse of the Tabernacle, and the punishment: Eli and his family would lose their hold on the Sanctuary, were to be doomed to eternal impoverishment, to begging for scraps and work from other priests.

A prediction easily as bad as any she had given, Cassandra expected the anger her own prophecies elicited. Yet Eli, what self-control! No wailing, no pleading, no offering bribes, saying only, "He is God; He will do what is good in His eyes."

Instinct had propelled her to her secluded spot, where she could safely vent her prophetic spleen, but it was a false alarm. The remembered half-scene had quieted her stomach and mind, with no information about Paris or his trip. A new torture, she decided. When she longed to be normal, they raped her throat, dragged words out of her mouth. Now that she wanted to know more, they abandoned her.

She spent the next week looking over her shoulder, wondering when the gods would ambush her with their message. Like a fugitive, she was always checking for a safe place to run, the quickest exit from any room she entered. Finally, tired of the looks that passed between the people who observed her behavior, she decided to wait out the gods at the port, where everyone always ignored her.

She went seeking only the peace of isolation but found comfort, the water soothing her stormy mind. Its rhythm spoke to her, encouraged her to roll with whatever came, to recognize how cyclical it all was.

Shipments came and left, messages reached their addressees and got their responses, sailors disembarked to carouse, reboarded for their next destination. Through it all, the water stayed. More or fewer waves, ships, or fish; through it all, the water sat serene, comfortable. It was what it was, the elixir of life, the grower of harvests, the bearer of ships and cargo. It did not *try* to be; it *was*.

Cassandra sat and listened and understood. Her distress was self-inflicted, the outcome of insisting she needed to change the future when her job was only to predict it. She had only to be, let the gods and history work out the rest. They are the gods; that which is good in their eyes they will do.

By the fourth week of her crash course in serenity, she had escaped her funk enough to notice the other woman who sat at the seaside each day.

"Hello. I'm Cassandra. You are?"

Not yet twenty, a girl really, pretty in the simple ways of the country, the other woman blushed and lowered her eyes. The material of her long white robe spoke of money and position, but was unadorned with the usual dyes and stones. Her hair, tied in a neat bun, also bore none of the appurtenances favored by the wealthy. The robe was a gift, Cassandra guessed, or a sign of recently moving up in life, maybe by marrying well.

"I'm Oenone, Paris' wife. No, don't apologize, no reason you should have remembered me; we met only that once at the celebration your father made for our return, and I'm sure you had other matters on your mind. I actually begged Paris to get the king to excuse you, but he…well, he wouldn't explain it to me, but he got very stubborn, insisted that, no, you had to be there, see him restored and the city standing."

Cassandra smiled to make clear how little Oenone needed to excuse herself, happy to wave aside thoughts of her brother and the future in the name of a budding friendship. There was no reason, she reminded herself, to visit the sins of the man on his innocent wife. "So you come to watch for him?"

She ducked her head again, a twitch Cassandra knew from others who had been forced to adapt to a new social class. "Not really, I just have nothing better to do. Paris was the only one I really knew in Troy, and now, with him gone…"

They made it a habit. Cassandra would wake, prove her sanity to her mother, gather any news or gossip, and make her way to the water. Oenone, still free of court obligations, would already be there, most often having packed lunch. They would sit and talk about this or that, or share the companionable silence of those with no place to go.

One delight of Oenone was how she quieted the background noise in Cassandra's head, almost as if the gods fled her company. Trusting their assessment, Cassandra relaxed, sharing frustrations she had never admitted to anyone else, allowing herself to voice her misery at a life derailed.

Much of the time, they focused on children, which both women enjoyed discussing. True to her roots, Oenone hoped for a large and spread-out brood, guaranteeing that at least a few would survive the gauntlet of early diseases and reach adulthood. Cassandra spoke of her despair, of the gods having sealed her marriage prospects and her womb.

Shaking her head, she said, "I guess it was not meant to be."

"Did you ask the gods to forgive you, to revoke their curse?"

Oenone's words were so unexpected, Cassandra at first misunderstood them. She told of her years trying to take matters into her own hands, bedding any willing man, trying for motherhood in whatever way possible. Oenone interrupted. "I wasn't suggesting *circumventing* the gods; I asked whether you *confronted* them, beseeched them to change their decree."

In the instant before Hannah reappeared in her mind, she only had time for the thought, *What an odd idea.* The Hebrew woman was standing before Eli at a building...the Sanctuary, Cassandra realized, since she could see the altar where Hofni and Pinhas had stood. Hannah was standing, eyes closed, lips moving, the High Priest looking at her with distaste. She was praying without voice, but Cassandra knew, as only another barren woman could, what inspired such focus. The dream let her hear Hannah promise to dedicate the boy to the Lord's service his whole life.

Cassandra watched with scorn, *As if such a simple deal would change a god's mind.* Yet the next moment she was watching Hannah bringing a young boy to the Sanctuary, telling Eli this was he for whom she had prayed. And closure, the last missing piece of the dream finally coming back, the boy growing, having his first prophecy in bed, not recognizing what it was, until Eli taught him to reply, "Speak, Lord, for your servant is listening."

The vision faded, but her eyes were wet as she hugged Oenone. "Thank you, thank you, thank you!"

"For what?"

"For showing me where I've gone wrong, what's missing, what I need to do!"

"Ask the gods for assistance?"

No one would ever know how their lives might have changed had the conversation continued. She would have had to take Oenone through her whole sordid history, but together they might have found the way to free her, to save Troy.

It was not meant to be. Oenone returned the hug, but her eyes stayed on the horizon, its setting sun still shooting red streaks into the sky. In front of those rays, there were dots, ships just coming into view. She pointed, and Cassandra knew even before she turned her head.

Like women said about pregnancy and childbirth, these last weeks of peace had been so calm as to make Cassandra forget the violence of a fit. The point of Oenone's finger brought it all back, warning of an outburst of greater force than she could remember, perhaps the strongest ever. She raced from the dock, hoping the bladder on her prophecy would not burst. Not since childhood and outhouse training had she felt such lack of control over her bodily processes.

She got away not a moment too soon. "Beware the one who returns, gone as one of two, arrives with another to complete him. The son cast out comes back, bringing destruction for him and all around him! Beware the one who returns, gone as one of two, arrives with another to complete him. The son cast out comes back, bringing destruction for him and all around him! Beware…"

For the first few repetitions, the prediction filled her whole head. Once she had memorized it, a part of her brain could turn to the problem of whom else to tell it to, since the gods would keep her mouth moving until she found a second permanent repository of these words.

"Cassandra, are you okay?" Oenone had come looking, concerned by her friend's rushed exit. Cassandra struggled to close her mouth, but once started, it could not be stopped for more than a few seconds. Had they met in the street, she could have squelched herself until she got past the now-thrust-aside wife. With Oenone waiting for an answer, there was no way.

"Beware the one who returns, gone as one of two, arrives with another to complete him. The son cast out comes back, bringing destruction for him and all around him! Beware the one who returns, gone as one of two, arrives with another to complete him. The son cast out comes back, bringing destruction for him and all around him! Beware…"

Neither of them would soon forget, so the compulsion faded, her self-control returning with each recitation. Cassandra swallowed back one or two repetitions trying to make their way into the world, and tried to apologize.

"I am so sorry. I tried to get away before it came out, but you came looking. Believe me, I am more embarrassed by my brother than you can know; I only wish he had realized what a mistake it would be to seek anyone other than you."

Oenone had relaxed at the beginning of the apology, stiffening again as she realized what her sister-in-law was saying. "You mean you think your ravings were true? It can't be! My Paris, throw me over for someone else? Who could he love more than me? The slopes of Ida testify that no one could come between us!"

Ye gods, Cassandra moaned as she felt the next wave coming, *why would they make her destroy every friendship?* No matter; the tornado inside would not be denied. "You speak of love, when he thinks of lust. You remember the simplicity of goodness, when he looks to widen his shadow on the world stage. Yea, there is love inside him, but the infatuation with beauty hides it until too late. Only when Oenone is lost to Paris forever will he know what he has lost. Your time with Paris is over; you can only save yourself by releasing him from your heart. You speak of love, when he thinks of lust. You remember…"

"Enough!!! You who have never felt a husband's regard, how dare you speak? Paris will return to me. Beauty lasts only so long, and then he will remember our bond. This is how you repay me, after I gave you love, affection, friendship, patience? You throw your bitterness at me? The gods will judge between you and me!!!"

And she stalked off, leaving Cassandra to mutter her way back to the city, to dump the still-repeating mantra on some poor soul not quick enough to flee a prophetess in the throes of her curse.

BOOK OF SAMUEL, CHAPTERS 4–8

As Menelaus massed the Greeks to secure the return of his wayward wife, King Priam took an unprecedented interest in his daughter's views of the situation.

"Cassandra, what are we supposed to do?"

"Father, I have told you what I have been told. Paris will ruin our city, our family, all we have worked to build and create. He carries the curse of the gods."

"What would you have me *do*?"

"I have not heard, but the solution seems clear. Return Helen with an apology and punish the fool who stole her. The Greeks would have no more cause for war, and we would return to normal. At least, most of us would."

This particular shake of her father's head, common to all parents who could not bring themselves to discipline a wayward child, had only begun with Paris' return. Her father, ruler of all Troy, would say this time and so many others, "Paris refuses."

The gods liked Priam's answer even less than Cassandra. "Hear me, king of Troy!!! Your intoxication with the newfound one will destroy your other children, as well as the citizens who look to you as father and king! Will you be so foolish as to waste the blessings of the gods to pander to the whims of the once-abandoned one? Take away his plaything, give him another distraction. Treat him as the child he is; he will forget Helen, as he forgot Oenone, as he will forget the bedmate of next year. Only stop him before he drags all else with him. Hear me, king of Troy..."

It ran its course, eventually, and she fell to the floor, drained; Priam himself rose, picked her up, and walk/carried her back to the throne, rocking her in a gesture of comfort she supposed went back to her infant days. "Ah, Cassandra, what are we going to do? He won't give her up, no matter how much I ask. Her husband won't accept any tribute without the return of his wife, and will soon, I fear, want the boy's head as well. What are we to do?"

She could only stare, her father's blind or stubborn denial too overwhelming.

Others would not or could not help. Hecuba suggested she convince Paris to return Helen, a conversation whose outcome any fool could predict. *Really, Mother,* Cassandra thought, *have you seen the woman?* A man would not tire of her even with the death-poison running through his veins; he would drag himself back to her bed for one last kiss.

She had thought Hector might see it her way, since he had the most to lose, but failed to reckon with the warrior's code. "I can't make him give her back! First, have you seen her?! Good for him, the little man; if I'd known such a one was available for plucking, I might have given him a run for her myself. Besides, who do these Spartans think they are, *demanding* her return? Let them try and compete with the might of Troy!

"Let them come and learn why we stand astride the Greek world, the standard of excellence for all cities. No, sister, this is not the time for Troy to turn tail and whimper. All of Hellas watches; when we repulse our attackers, they will learn our power! Honor demands we support our brother; politics urges us to take our place at the forefront of the cities of Greece!"

51

As he spoke, in her mind she saw him tied to the back of a chariot, being dragged around the walls of the city. When it sat calmly in her head, her relief at not having to shout it out expressed itself in a hug, the first she had given him since he left the children's wing so many years before, graduated to soldier and commander. "Hector, do you know I love you?"

He put some of his well-known strength into the hug, patting her back as he did, without any of the pique that usually came with his being cut off in the middle of a speech. "Don't worry; we know how to handle this. This will blow over; your fits will subside; it will all work out. Thirty years from now, you and I will sit around watching our grandchildren play and fight."

This time, the gods were good to her; the montage of visions that burst into her head did her the favor of staying serenely there, with no push to be articulated. She saw the boy prophet, Samuel, making a name for himself, telling people whatever they needed to know, always emphasizing that his information came from their god, and that they could find out whatever they wanted from that god. She saw him a little older, the people more in awe of him now than before, drawing back as he walked.

Then, the last picture, Samuel—now a young man— wandering the land, calling the people to war. A war, she saw on his face, he knew they could not win, but which the god had decided they must fight.

A war they could not win, but the god had decided they must fight. That must be the message for her, told her what she had to do in this conversation. "Hector, you're right. War is your business, and I should leave you to it. I'm sorry for trying to interfere."

Hector's self-confidence meant that what might to others seem an abrupt and unconvincingly sudden change of heart to him seemed like her coming to her senses. He walked off, swagger slightly more pronounced for having been told that his sister, she who always knew better, recognized his superior military capabilities.

The vision continued after Hector left, giving her the grim satisfaction of knowing that Samuel would also have to stand by, watching his Hebrews lose, as she would have to watch Troy. It was all happening in her head, but she was so caught up, she physically leaned forward, anxious to see how the Hebrew prophet would react.

Nothing. He continued living his life, as if he did not know the enemy had destroyed their leaders, killed many of their citizens, taken the Ark of their Covenant with their god. Nor did he react to the epidemic that struck the enemy, or to their deciding they were supposed to return the Ark, or to the Hebrews moving it around as they tried to find a place it would produce blessing rather than plague or death.

And Samuel was quiet this whole time. No one consulted him, and he continued his own path, , following his routine, wandering the country, sharing his god's words with those who asked, saying nothing about the major issues of the day. Twenty years, *twenty years* before he stepped in to take charge.

The vision closed, but Cassandra was sure she had gotten it this time. If it takes years for the people to come around, that's what it takes. She could wait as well as Samuel.

BOOK OF SAMUEL, CHAPTERS 8–15

Ten years later, realization crashed through her defenses. It had been nibbling away for months, or years, but finally she could no longer hush it: there would not be enough time. The siege wore away at the people; every month she heard more snapping and sniping among her fellow citizens; the plentiful stores of food and weapons could not fortify their patience. She would not have twenty years.

The gods had been waiting for this opening, since that night she had her first vision of the siege. Her last thoughts were about the city's inability to hold out, and she dreamt of Samuel objecting to the people's desire for a king. Objecting? She snorted in her sleep. It took a special kind of idiot to be upset at being relieved of responsibilities.

Upon waking, she shook her head at his pettiness, his taking offense at their wanting a military man to fight the king of Ammon. *Sounds about right,* she mused. *You want words of the gods, go to a prophet; you want military victory, go to a general.*

A trap the gods had laid for her, their retort springing up in return. *Oh, yeah? You're so much better? How much support have you given Hector these past years?*

It was time to go see her brother.

The war had been good to him, firming his hold on the future throne, molding him further in their father's image. The job of a leader, Priam said as often as anyone would listen, was to keep the citizens happy and in a positive frame of mind. Once you commit to a path, you follow it through to the end. Surrendering or admitting defeat demoralized people, and leaders never demoralize.

She went to offer support to what she thought would be a privately demoralized brother, only to find him still confident of victory. Her resolve melted as he spoke of the city's defenses, until finally, she had to say, "Hector, can you not see that you must abandon this... madness! Paris has had ten years of this woman; it is enough. Let him give her back with an apology. For all of our sakes, can he not relinquish her to her rightful husband?"

Hector had drunk his father's juice, and was not interested in negative thoughts. Making no secret of the anger he was holding in, he said, his tone barely even, "Look, you have to stay out of business that's not yours. The war is going well, all told. Our supplies are strong, our spies foster strife and dissension; when their allies begin leaving, we'll take the war out to them, and then we'll show 'em a thing or two."

Her last coherent thought before waking on the ground was that no god could obligate her to accept such absurdities. The next she knew, Hector was standing over her, patting her cheeks, trying to revive her.

"Cassandra? Cassandra, can you hear me? Cassandra, it's me, Hector!" Pat, pat, pat. As soon as she could focus enough to put her arms in motion, she raised them to stop the rhythmic slaps on her face. Her brother knew a lot, but not his own strength.

"Hector, yes, stop, I'm...Hector!" He paused. "I'm fine, yes, please stop! What happened?" She was stretched out, as far as she could tell, exactly where she had been standing, as if her legs had given way, and she had simply dropped.

He shook his head back and forth. "I don't know. You were standing there, I was talking, and then you got this sort of faraway look, like you were thinking, and then you nodded, as if agreeing with yourself, and then you opened your mouth.

"Next thing I know, you've bent your knees and lain yourself straight out on the ground, yammering about some guy not waiting. You were calling out to him, 'Wait! Wait! Wait!' and then you stopped for a minute, and then again you started calling out, to kill them all, that leaving the animals alive would be a mistake. I didn't know what to do, really, because in your fits, we never stop you, but this wasn't like a fit..."

Didn't feel like a fit, either, she thought, as she checked the body parts generally mistreated during an episode. Fits also did not put her on the floor, nor did she need to be brought back to consciousness. More like the dreams, but this was during the day.

Whatever it was, she knew what she had seen and its message. Getting Hector to understand it would be a more daunting task. Looking him in the eye, she said, "I have to tell you something, and it will sound strange."

He raised an eyebrow, a hint of a smile around his lips. "Strange? From you? Shocking!"

She laughed, delighted. It had been too long since he had made a joke and was an excellent beginning. "Just after Paris came back, I started having visions in my sleep."

"You mean outbursts at night?"

"No, these were different...more gentle, no yelling or thrashing or anything like that. It's like regular dreams, but they told a story about some nation I've never heard of, the Hebrews. When these...visions started, there seemed to be parallels between our situation and theirs, as if we're supposed to learn from them."

Hector stood up to pace, arms behind his back, brow furrowed, as if he were reviewing the troops or consulting with his top commanders. "Do you mean these dreams have morals, like a fable?"

"Not in so many words, but yes, the morals of the stories seemed clear to me."

His brow went from furrow to frown. "Not to insult you, but why would I believe the dreams any more than the fits?"

She had known the question was coming, not if she could answer it. "If you hear how they started, I think you'll see why."

"Okay."

The image was as vivid now as when they had been... together. He had not been the first of her lovers to meet a tragic end, or even the first whom the gods forced her to tell of his coming doom. He had differed in being the first she cared about for reasons other than his value as bedmate and sperm donor.

"I don't know how well you remember my...activities before Paris returned, but there was a time when I was less than...selective with my affections."

She knew Hector hated speaking of that period in her life; to him, it was a reminder of his failure to have been a more positive influence on her. In his simple world, more brotherly love might have meant less promiscuity. Teeth clenched behind closed lips, he nodded, waving her to continue.

"Well, there was this one fellow I called Mr. Three, because he always..."

"Go on, go on, I don't need to know why."

His impatience didn't help. She swallowed twice, but her voice still came out as a squeak. She reached for a nearby flask, drank a bit, and continued. "Anyway, the next morning, I was waking up, and the previous night's…pleasures stopped me from being as aware of my symptoms as usual, so I was caught almost totally by surprise. I remember I was thinking he wasn't much to look at, average height, had cropped his hair too short, and the bump of his nose would have turned me off, if not for his compensating qualities. So there I was, clucking to myself over how the ones from whom you expect the least turn out to be the best, and then it hit."

He knew her well enough to know what that meant. "A fit?"

"And a doozy." This was one of the few times she was glad the outbursts forced her to memorize, as the words sprang lightly into her head. She struck a pose, so Hector would know she was replaying the scene. "Man of my bed, heed my words! Beware the ones you call allies, for they mean you no good. The head you hold so high will soon roll on the ground; the arms that caress women will soon lay dead in Mother Earth; the legs that wrap around your lovers, severed from the body, thrown afar; the tongue that sits in your mouth will roll in the dust."

Hector whistled, sympathizing with how that would come off the morning after. Shaking his head at his sister's trials in life, he interrupted, "I get it. So you had this outburst, and what happened? How'd he take it?"

Cassandra bit back a snappy retort at his readiness to interrupt her, despite how annoying she found it in the reverse. It was good, all told, that he was so intent on her story. "He was so surprised, it took a few repetitions before he absorbed what I was saying. Then, of course, he did what everyone else does, got mad at me. He cursed me out, saying if I wanted to get rid of him, I should just say so, made some snide comments about our time together, and then stormed off."

Hector had been expecting more, losing interest at the banal turn of events. "This has a point, right? Because I've got a training session, a strategy conference, and a shift of guard duty on the walls, so if we could move this along…"

"All right, all right, I'm getting there. The point is, he stormed *back* in, ranting about how if I thought I was such a great prophet, why didn't I do more than harbinger doom, why didn't I find ways to help people *avoid* their fate? So I said, 'Like it's so easy changing what comes out of my mouth! You think I like doing this? You think I *want* to scare off every man I meet?' But he went toe-to-toe, something about how I should stop thinking of myself as a pawn, find ways to change the future by changing the people, or some such."

Hector's impatience had him punching a fist into his open hand. "Your point?"

"My point is he got me wondering, thinking, looking around. And I found out about these people, the Hebrews, how their prophets always told them their actions could affect what happened to them. And I figured, if I could hook up with *their* god, well, who knows what could happen? So—and this you'll remember because Mother and Father were almost ready to have me committed—I stayed in my room whenever I could, closed off all my other activities, and focused on that god."

"And it worked?"

She nodded, hoping he was fully roped in; if he believed her, Troy might yet survive. "Least I think it did, because I started having these dreams the night after Paris came back. At first, I didn't even know what it was, almost went out of my head with worry that the gods had decided to give me outbursts day and night. When I got past that, I realized I was being shown one of the Hebrew prophets, named Samuel. I had a few then, a few more when he took Helen and war was brewing, but then not for the past ten years. The thing is, though, they always come when they connect to something going on *right then!*"

Hector let the silence hang between them. "And just now was your latest."

She nodded. "Yes."

"Do I want to know what it said?"

"Want to? Tough question. Ought to? Absolutely."

Hector sighed, sat himself on a stone, shoulders already slumping under the weight of the anticipated burden. Once he was ready, she took one more breath. "All right, leaving out the smaller parts, there's this Hebrew people with a prophet, Samuel…" She told him of the high hopes at Saul's coronation, too quickly followed by a misstep, failing to follow Samuel's directions about when to offer a particular sacrifice.

Then, the final tragedy, the Amalek fiasco, where Saul again refused or neglected to follow orders, this time to annihilate an ancient enemy—men, women, children, and all possessions. She told the story straight, trying to be brief, expecting understanding to come to her brother's face. When she finished, he sat there, waiting for more.

"And?"

"What do you mean, "And?" That's it."

"I thought you said it was relevant to me or to Troy."

"It was; I mean it *is*. Don't you see? Look, let me say it this way. When this war started, I had visions of Samuel objecting to the people getting a king, getting their own independent military leader. I thought it was his ego, that he was getting full of himself. I didn't want to be like that, so I came and apologized, said to handle the war your way.

"But I was wrong; that's what this vision was showing me. Saul succeeded only when he listened to Samuel."

Now that he was getting her point, he wasn't getting any happier. "Are you saying...that you think...that we should fight this war in consultation with...you?"

This was a dangerous question, especially knowing Hector; it would need a careful answer. Too many people, in Troy and out, were power hungry; if she smelled of that, she'd miss her chance again. "I'm not saying it for any thrills I get out of it; I'm just telling you that if my whatever-you-want-to-call-it means anything, it means that."

Hector was on the line, not able to accept her claim, but not able to reject it, either. "All right, so what should we do?"

She waited, expecting the message to hit, for her to find herself again laid out on the floor, but nothing happened. Meaning, she supposed, she had all the information she needed, especially when memory flashed a picture of Hector's corpse being dragged around the city's walls. If only she could say it right.

"Look. I know I sometimes sound crazy; I know I've opposed the war; I know you think it's going well. But, and please, please, please, think about what I'm saying!!! I *know* that if this war continues, everyone we love—you, Father, Mother, Paris, any member of the family you name—will die or be taken captive. If we end it, none of that will be true."

As if he had expected this but hoped for something else, he stood, shaking his head in disappointment and turned to the door. Desperate now, she called, "Hector!"

He came all the way back and folded her in a warm embrace. As he gently kissed the top of her head, he whispered, barely loudly enough to be heard, "You may be right, Cassandra, your dreams may tell the truth; who knows? But the die is cast. My duty is to father and lord. The gods give us our roles to play in this world, as you of all people know, and we cannot always choose where we end up. Please don't say more; it's already hard enough. Think well of me, and know I always did as the gods required."

His belief in her, fatalistic as it was, inspired a sense of determined resistance new to Cassandra. Her jaw was unaccustomed to setting itself for a fight with Fate, but there was no way she would let Hector go gently to his death. Clueless as to how to go about doing it, the first step was securing a vision, one that told her what *she* wanted to know, not what some god or other decided to tell her.

That part, at least, she knew how to handle, and Hector was barely out the door before she was mentally ticking off what she needed. Early to bed and wake before sunrise, either to record the night's dream or to have time for a solid early morning trance.

She would need a lock for the door, for those mornings the first two tries failed; she could not risk Mother or Father hearing that their daughter had been pacing her room, calling, "God of Samuel, speak to me."

She pushed to her feet. The grains of sand were dropping in the glass, and time was running out.

BOOK OF SAMUEL, CHAPTERS 16–24

Knowing progress would be slow, that the vision she sought might take months to come, did not lessen her agony as she waited. She could sense each second passing, knew it brought closer the end of the world as she knew it.

The morning her father's guards arrived to shepherd her to the walls of the city, she had been lying in bed, nailing down each detail of the vision that had finally come the previous night, wanting to be sure she said it exactly as she had seen it.

Their knock and call, "Miss Cassandra, your father says you are to come with us!" muscled all other thoughts out of her head, sparking a buzz of anxiety that shoved away any other coherent reaction. They took her to her father's viewing point atop the city's walls, where he stood sweeping his eyes over the expanse of field that separated Troy from the enemy camp. Down there, in the no-man's-land where there were occasional skirmishes, stood a man, head thrown back with the casual arrogance of the supremely confident, waiting, eyes on the city.

She would adhere to the minimal standards of civility, but no more than that. "Majesty."

"Ah, Cassandra!!! Come watch your brother bring victory to Troy."

"Brother? Which brother?" Her mind supplied the answer before her father did: *As if he would do them all a favor and send Paris to a real battle.*

"Hector. He goes to yonder Achilles; when he beats him, we shall finally rid ourselves of these pesky armies."

How could they both be so stupid? The words were not a thought; they were the refrain of the elegy that was her life. She had told them and told them and told them. Hector could not save the city, certainly could not beat Achilles.

There had to be a way to get them to listen, and the dream must have the answer. It had been of a boy, walking out of *his* army encampment toward a giant waiting for him. As she had looked closer in her sleep, to see him better, the scene shifted to show Samuel sneaking in to Bethlehem to anoint the young David.

She noted first that he was the little guy, not the strongest or the best warrior. Not Hector for sure; that must be the answer. Only a little guy could kill Achilles; putting anyone else up meant death. About to open her mouth to tell her father so, the prayer sprang to her lips, "God of Samuel, help my words, so I can save my beloved brother."

She took one more moment to try for as firm a hold on herself as she could muster. She got as far as "Father" before the gods intervened. "Fool of a man, travesty of a king! Your stubbornness sends your firstborn to his death. God has chosen another; insisting on this battle seals his needless fate. When will you listen to me, king of Troy? How long can you last, setting your path counter to the gods'?"

A shout went up as Hector emerged from the gates, diverting Priam, closing off any answer. Instead, he turned to lead the assembled crowd in cheers for their favorite son, trying to outdo the masses on the other side making similar noise for Achilles.

She understood that he expected her to step forward and join him in watching the outcome. Steeling herself, she closed her eyes to find that Hector's progress appeared on the insides of her lids as vividly as if her eyes were open.

Worse, as he walked, her vision split in two, so that she saw *two* men walking across a field to battle the champion of the larger, stronger enemy. On the right, her heavily armored brother, tall and broad, to all appearances certain he would bring glory to Troy, approaching his physically similar opponent. And on the left, David, ordinary clothing, sling his only weapon, walking with eyes down, scanning the ground as he approached the waiting Goliath.

Knowing the end of each of the scenes, she cursed the fate that would make her watch her brother die, wondered why she had not been shown a way to save him. Instantly with the thought, the vision changed, replaying the hour before David went out to his battle. Goliath was in the middle of the field, calling for a challenger, and the boy was wandering through the Hebrew camp, stopping soldier after soldier.

"Who is yonder giant, who reviles the armies of the Living God of Israel?"

"That's Goliath, the champion of the Philistines."

"And what does he want, this man who blasphemes and ridicules the Living God?"

"He's calling for a challenger, and the king has said that he'll give his daughter in marriage to whoever kills him. But who would be mad enough to go to certain death?"

David again: "I would; for who is he, to revile, blaspheme, and ridicule the hosts of the Living God?"

As the dream showed her repeated incidents of the exchange, time slipping away as Hector made the long trek to his death, Cassandra urged it to hurry and get to the point. It stayed stuck, showing her the same conversation, over and over. Even when David got to Saul and offered to take up the challenge, he seemed less interested in the reward, or the battle, than mentioning his god and all the other battles He had helped him win. He had killed a lion, a bear; his god had helped him with all that, she got that, but so what?

The vision jumped back to David bending to fill his sack with stones from the riverbed, as Hector neared Achilles. That time was passing at equal speed on both sides of her mind told her she had scant moments to figure out what she was being told.

The people! David involved others; that must be it! Stepping back with care, watching to be sure neither her father nor his retinue was aware of her movements, she moved out of the royal viewing stand, trying to get out of eye- and earshot as quickly as possible.

As soon as she was free, she tried to start a chant on the walls. "Bring back Hector! Bring back Hector!"

Surprised to hear something other than "Go, Hector, Troy stands behind you!" several people paused to stare at her. She focused on them, yelling, "Hector cannot beat Achilles, I swear it! We can save his life by recalling him! There is a way for all of us to survive, to save our city, but this is not it. We must act now, or it will be too late, his life will be lost forever. Bring back Hector! Bring back Hector!"

His death walk took perhaps a quarter of an hour more, time she used to try six spots, failing to move any of the people from their mad certainty that he could win. As she gave up, she noticed David's scene had gotten a little ahead. Hector and Achilles were still facing each other from about ten paces, sizing up strengths and weaknesses, making feints with their swords that the opponent could largely ignore.

David, on the other hand, was busy giving a speech. "You come to me with a sword, a spear, and a club, and I come to you in the name of the Lord of Hosts, the God of the camps of Israel, whom you have reviled."

His words had no chance to register because she was too busy watching her brother, hoping he would yet find a way to live, knowing he would not. David circled the sling overhead, shot out the stone, and saw it find the open spot in the giant's armor and knock him to the ground, unconscious. The way the two scenes played in her head, David's sword killing Goliath could almost have been the signal for Hector to strike at Achilles.

In the first moments, the Trojans still cheered loudly, expecting victory. After a few parries, fakes, and missed lunges, Hector caught Achilles full in the chest with his club, his sword ready for when the Greek dropped his defenses from the force of the blow. The noise on the walls edged up a notch, sure the end was near.

Cassandra shut her eyes tighter, caught in wishing he might win despite knowing the crash of disappointment to come. Achilles stepped back, shrugged off the blow as if a child had slapped him in anger, and then moved forward, ready to resume. His easy recovery from Hector's best sent a sigh of defeat through the crowd on the walls, the truth of Achilles' military superiority finally dawning on all assembled.

She prayed that at the very least death would come quickly, that her brother would not turn tail and flee like some common coward. That too was denied her. Grief made its way across the walls, all of Troy knowing there was no outrunning Achilles in battle.

The denouement came on the winged feet of all tragedy. Vivid as it was in her mind, it would be worse if she opened her eyes. Achilles caught Hector, tied him to the back of his chariot, dragged him around the city walls, and took his time about killing him as an object lesson to the city that thought it could resist the massed might of Greece.

She ran back to the royal viewing stand, knowing she had one last duty to discharge that day. There were new age lines in her father's face, which neither surprised nor moved her. Priam would feel the loss of his declared heir, to be sure, but he recovered well and fast. If she knew her father, he'd return to full strength in a year or two. And Hector would still be dead.

Hector dead; the words in her mind unlocked her lips. She had been hoping to throw an outburst at him, but got only silence from the gods. She was on her own.

"When will you learn? Reap the harvest of ignoring me, Father! Know this, and never forget—your son is dead because of you. And as you lead this city to defeat, to everlasting shame as the polis so blind it could not see its need to surrender, know too that all the suffering, the disease, the slavery, and the death that draw ever closer, all rest on your shoulders."

Priam nodded his head, patted her on hers, but did not say anything as he moved to return to the palace, followed by a retinue overcome with grief and shock. Reaching the edge of the observation nook, he turned.

"You may be right, daughter, you may be right. It does not matter anymore. My life ended today; others will see this through. The gods have rendered their judgment and found me wanting. I accept their punishment, and will withdraw from public life. Henceforth, bring your prophecies to Paris."

She stood there openmouthed, trying not to believe he would compound his stupidity by abdicating in Paris' favor. Even Paris would have to see the madness in that, would have to ask his father to find a more suitable candidate.

She ran to her last living brother's quarters, but he wasn't there. The beauty who answered the door told her she had no idea where he had gone, had not seen him since...well, regardless of how she said it, she meant that morning, about twenty minutes after they both awoke.

Feeling the gods had lured her here for *some* reason, she asked the nearest woman, a vagrant or a peddler, if she'd seen Paris. "Didn'tja hear? The king's sent messengers to the Greeks to request the return of Hector's body for the funeral pyre. Paris musta gone with 'em, is what I'm thinkin'."

The flood of images hit Cassandra so quickly, she had no choice but to sit down where she stood, to sort them out. Most people managed to get around her, but she later found a few bruises from those not nimble enough to avoid stepping on the madwoman crouching in a public thoroughfare.

She saw Paris walking, not *with* the messengers, but skulking along on the side, shooting Achilles. The arrow hit him in the heel, his one weak spot, felling and killing him. The scene shifted, to Paris raising his arms in triumph, taking his brother's place at the head of the army as the enraged Greeks charged the swooping Trojans, his need to prove himself luring him from his usual safe position in the back, with the archers.

Perhaps he's our David, the thought came, only for the vision to show her an arrow strike him in *his* heel, shocking her as much as him.

69

The vision of her younger brother facing death wrenched her heart, even as she also felt the satisfaction of being vindicated. Paris dragged himself all the way to Mount Ida, the slow-acting poison weakening him with each step, to find Oenone, his first love, the only mortal with the antidote.

Futile as it was, Cassandra found herself praying Oenone would yield and cure him. Surely she would believe his promise to get rid of Helen, to return to her, to try to make up for the pain he had caused his one true love. But no, his recognition of the folly of throwing away innocence and emotional connection on the altar of beauty and prestige had come fatally late. Oenone's bitterness won out over the love she could not eradicate from her heart. She cradled him, crying as his last breaths took away all she had ever wanted, beginning the mourning that would consume the rest of her childless years.

Cassandra slapped away a tear as the vision faded. What a weakling she was, feeling pity for the one who had caused so much pain, loss, death, and destruction! She could not even take solace in the hope that losing two generals in a day would convince the people to give up the war, because she knew her father too well. His sons' deaths would awaken his sense of obligation, renew his energies to avenge them, to restore the honor of the city.

She did not need to join the futile game; for her it would end here. She dragged her feet back to her room. If she stayed there and did nothing, perhaps the gods would allow it. She could concede, give up, resign herself, whatever they wanted. They were the gods; that which was good in their eyes they would do.

BOOK OF SAMUEL CHAPTERS 25–26

Weeks later, she was woken by a throbbing that intensified every second she did not leave her room. Having fallen out of practice at handling such compulsions, she barely managed to dress before being expelled from her chamber. Half walking, half tripping down streets lightening with the advancing dawn, she was surprised to see others headed in the same direction.

She asked a couple where they were going, got the sneering, "You're the prophet; you should know!!!"

Yeah, good one, like I've never heard that before.

She tried walking the other way, but the pounding returned in full force. Following the crowd, she turned the final corner, stepped up on the wall where the people were congregated, followed the arc of their eyes, and found the answers she sought. Victory or defeat, the horse would end this.

Its size astounded her. Although she was standing atop walls Poseidon and Apollo had built so high as to be insurmountable, its eyes looked into her own. She stretched her hand out to touch it, only to feel ridiculous for having forgotten the illusion of distance. Big as it was, it was still far away.

Her mother was already there, watching the debate swirling around the king. Cassandra gave the required hug and kiss and asked what was going on.

"They're trying to figure out what to do with it."

Her stomach began to rumble, as she had expected it would. The gods sent her among the people for only one reason. "Do with it?"

"Most people seem to think the Greeks left this as an apology to Apollo; the ships have sailed, so it seems like it's over. *They* say open the gates and bring it to the Temple, part of our victory celebration."

Bad idea, bad idea, bad idea!!! Her insides screamed the phrase, turned it into a mantra she could not stop or pause. She weighed each word before she let it out of her mouth, ready to clamp and bolt should the madness come. "And the other side?"

"Well, they're not even a group, a few cranks really, but they suggest it's a trap."

A trap, that's it!!! The click in her head told her how well the cranks had seen through the charade, had figured out the Greeks' idea. What kind of trap? How would it work? The immediate silence, normally a relief, was no surprise. How she had not missed these fits! As always, the gods gave her enough information to annoy those around her, not enough to let her convince them they should follow her.

The moment approached; to her dismay, it was coupled with the irresistible need to present herself to her father, deliver her words to him. She called back her apology to Hecuba, whom she'd left in midsentence, promising to return as soon as she could.

She had not seen him since the day of Hector's death. Despite his many summonses and pleas, she had skipped all public, formal, or official ceremonies, including Paris and Hector's joint funeral pyre. That he had not ordered her to attend suggested that her mother had accurately portrayed the war's recent toll on him.

His hair and beard were wild, not having been trimmed perhaps since—was she so weak that he could still arouse her sympathy?—she had pointed the finger at him for his son's death. The lines on his face were deeper and more plentiful than she remembered, and the rings of exhaustion around his eyes made him seem to peer out at the world from holes in his skull.

From those depths, the fire still raged. Terrible as the cost had been, she could see how he yet thought he could succeed, no, thought he *had* succeeded. Cassandra had heard him say it so many times, but had not understood its full meaning until now. He had convinced himself that this disaster would make him immortal. In three thousand years, he had often told Hector, their war would still be spoken of all over the world.

Catching sight of her, the flame in his eyes burned in her direction. "Ah, Cassandra, my beautiful one, my pessimist, always certain of our defeat. What say you now, daughter, when the embodiment of our victory sits right outside our gates, when the Greek ships can be seen receding along the horizon?"

With silence from the gods, she gathered her wits. *Stress that it's a trap, that the Greeks would never give up when they have not suffered a single major loss, that we could see whether it's a trap by leaving the Horse for a few days, give the Greeks' plan a chance to unfold.* She could even assure them the gods would overlook this disrespect; being a prophet had to have some advantages.

Trap, Greeks, test, no offense to the gods. With the foolishness of the insistently naive, she opened her mouth, ready to logically and calmly win him and the rest of the Trojans over to her point of view. As the gods' words instead came flying out of her mouth, she was left only with enough mental space to curse herself for again falling for their trick.

"This horse spells the end of Troy! Hark, proud ones who refuse to accept our warnings! Your offering will turn upon you; Greeks will run through this city, the horse leading the way! Your women and children will be theirs, your gold and silver taken to line their streets and temples, your celebration of Apollo turning into theirs of Zeus and Hera!!! Troy will never listen, Troy will never learn, Troy will not last!!!"

She had delivered this same message before without effect, and there was nothing new here to suggest it would find a wider audience. Shame flooded her, embarrassment at still not having learned how to speak so others would listen. Too distraught to watch, she kept her eyes on the ground.

When the silence continued, she looked up, to find the crowd wavering, unsure of how to react. One by one, the few who had opposed bringing in the Horse came to stand with her, deciding she was the leader to follow. The proponents of opening the gates had fallen silent, trying to gauge the crowd's reaction.

Having moved to her side, Laocoon stepped in. "Trojans, have we not ignored Cassandra long enough? The gods sent us a guide, and we have insulted her, or worse, these long years, have instead followed Paris, to war, privation, and death.

"Now he is gone, Hector is gone, and the glory of our city is almost gone. We stand at a crossroads, either on the verge of victory," he nodded toward the proponents of that view, "or about to fall for the Greek trap. If it were just my word against theirs, Trojans, you would have a democratic choice to make. But here we have a prophetess of the gods, warning us. When will we finally heed her?"

His calm and collected presentation, what she so wished she could do, worked, drawing many from the crowd to Laocoon's side.

The gods would not allow it; the point of her torment was that she be ignored as she told the truth, not that others help her. Two serpents rose from the ground, as if created for that very purpose. Coiling themselves around him, they sank their fangs, each depositing its venom in one of his forearms.

To his credit, Laocoon did not panic. Falling to his knees, he pulled his knife from his belt, killed one serpent and wounded the other so that it released him and slunk away, scattering people as it slithered into the ocean. Once the danger was gone, he began sucking blood out of the wounds and spitting it onto the ground, trying to get the poison out.

Futile as Cassandra knew it to be, she rushed over to take the other arm and imitate him. He weakened; when the gods send serpents, death is near and certain. The strength leaving him, he fell full length on the ground, arms at his sides. His sight fading as his life ebbed away, Laocoon took the arm of the crying woman kneeling over him.

"Cassandra, forgive me, forgive us, we knew not what we did!"

No one had ever asked this of her. Thinking of what Samuel or David would have said, she placed her hand on his forehead, trying to cool the raging fever, and whispered, "There is nothing to forgive. Go in peace, and may your repose be peaceful."

Gratified by the small smile that registered on his lips before he breathed his last, she looked away, unable to bear the sight of yet another in the string of unnecessary losses the city would suffer.

Priam led the rush to open the gates, Laocoon's death proving to them that the gods had been displeased with him and all who followed him. Cassandra went to await the end where this had all started, in Apollo's Temple, the night she and Helenus had gotten locked in.

Ah, Helenus, how much better life was when I had a twin around, she sighed as she walked. They were six years old, ready to leave the palace on their own at night. After the children's wing darkened, they waited for Hector to get out of bed, check all the children, and lie down again. Once his breathing got that regular sound, they knew, no one else would be up.

Hector liked to pretend he was in charge because he was already *ten,* so he never let himself fall asleep until he'd ensured the others were already dreaming. Helenus and Cassandra agreed that for all his showing off, he envied them. Did he think they'd believe his fake excitement about spending the entire day perfecting his wrestling, spear-throwing, and swordplay? Poor Hector, they called him, doomed to be the good son, always doing as he was told.

The adult Cassandra, remembering, repeated the words, the lump in her throat keeping them from being audible. *Poor Hector, always doing as he was told.*

When they had gotten to the Temple, it was late and almost empty, but they still had to be sure no one saw them come in. Patience through anxious minutes paid off; an elderly gentleman opened the door wide as he left, too oblivious to notice them catching it before it closed. Long minutes in the foyer that led to the Sanctuary itself did not offer any similar opportunity. They agreed to risk it, struggling together to open the big wooden door enough to allow them to slip in.

The familiar room felt different at night. When Mother took them, they would hang on to her skirts, acting bashful around new people, turning their eyes away when the blood spewed from the pigs slaughtered on the altar at the front of the room. But now! They felt so big, coming to speak to the gods themselves.

The room was not only quieter than during the day, it was spookier, lit only by a few candles left from the nighttime prayers. Cassandra reached out for her brother's arm.

"'Lenus, I'm scared."

When they were alone, he wouldn't pretend in the way expected of him in public. He gulped and nodded.

"Me too, but if we turn back now, we're cowards."

A noise sent them scurrying, the fear of their parents catching them outside the palace worse than any terror the Temple itself might hold. As they watched, nudging each other to quiet down when their breath got too loud, two pairs of legs walked the room, pausing here and there to extinguish a candle or douse a bowl of incense. Work done, the legs returned to the door, and left.

"Now, I'm *really* scared." It had been bad enough when the room was lit; with only moonlight and shadows to see by, Cassandra's nerves shrilled at a new octave. She tried reminding herself that it was only the angle of the light, but the gigantic shadows of mice running along the walls convinced her that her parents were right. Six *was* too young to come here on her own, especially when it was deserted.

She turned to her brother. "I've had enough. I'm going home."

"You promised! Besides, if they catch you, they'll catch me!"

She ignored him, running up the rows to the door at the top. Pushing thoughtlessly, she fell backward when it stood firm. Surprised more than worried, she tried again, this time putting more effort into it. It gave hardly at all.

"Come here and help me."

"Help you?! When you're going home to get me in trouble?"

Brothers, even a twin, could be such a bother. "If you do, I'll stay with you until you fall asleep." No answer. "And cover for you if you get caught."

Grumbling about the burden of twins, females in particular, he joined her at the door, putting his shoulder into it, to no avail.

Eyes widening, she said, "Do you think they lock the Temple at night?"

His slapping his forehead was a signature gesture, the way he expressed his quick exasperation at obtuseness, his or anyone else's. "Of course! They lock the Temple at night, how could I be so dumb? Cass, I'm afraid we're locked in."

That was her first moment of real terror, the go-out-of-your-mind-with-anxiety kind. She raced around the room, looking everywhere for a hidden door, a window, access to the roof. Crying, wailing, banging on the door, she gave up only after exhausting herself, and then lay whimpering next to Helenus, holding his hand.

"Well, well, what have we here? Lost children?"

She blinked her eyes open to see a man, no, a god. Even as a little girl, she recognized the beauty rare in Troy, perhaps in all of Greece. As her eyes moved from the floor to his head, she picked out all the body parts her mother's gossip circle would have chattered about. The calf muscles, strong as they were, were overshadowed by the thighs only half-covered by his skirt.

Between the thighs and his stomach was the mysterious place the women only hinted at, but she had seen the bulge that must be the focus of all their tittering, the memory of which made the adult Cassandra shake her head with regret. Above, his tunic was pulled tight and fastened in back, to better delineate every ridge of his stomach.

She hadn't known then why muscles mattered. Her adult self relived the memory with a stirring of the sensuality she had suppressed these last years. At the time, she had latched on to his face, strong and powerful. Mesmerized as she had been, she had focused on the lips, full and red, asking her a question.

"How did you get in here?"

Her thoughts exactly. "How did *you* get in here?"

He squatted down to get as close to her level as possible. "Why, it's Cassandra, Priam and Hecuba's daughter! What a beautiful little girl! If Zeus grants you a body to match your face, you will be blessed indeed."

Taken aback that a stranger had known her by sight, she still had the presence of mind to take umbrage at his casual use of her parents' names. "That's His and Her Majesty to you, I believe."

He threw his head back and laughed. "A feisty one! Good for you, princess of Troy. Keep that spirit alive, and you'll go far, I guarantee you that."

Becoming more alert as the conversation continued, she noticed that the moonlight had gone, but the man had lit one of the candles. It must be getting on toward morning. "But you didn't answer me; how did *you* get in here?"

"Why, I live here, Cassandra, didn't you know that?"

"What do you mean? No one lives here, this is Apollo's Temple." When he smiled and nodded, her eyes grew wide. "You mean, you're…"

He widened his eyes, a gesture she took as confirmation, and she ran into his arms. "Oh, Apollo, I was so scared! We came here to worship, because now we're six and big, but then we got locked in for the night, and Helenus, he can sleep through anything, but I was crying, and I almost didn't fall asleep the whole night."

He sat her on his lap, and said, "Well, I'm here now, and nothing will happen to you. Why don't you relax for a bit, and then you can go back and sleep next to your brother, knowing that I'm watching over the two of you."

Sniffling back the tears that had accompanied her tale of woe, she said, "And Mother and Father and Hector and all the others, will you watch them too?"

He smoothed her hair, hugged her once tightly, and gave her a kiss on the cheek. "Not as closely as I will watch you, my pretty one, but I will do my best." Comforted, she nestled in his shoulder and drifted into a dreamless sleep.

As the memory faded, the adult Cassandra shook her head at what was the first step of her ruined life. Reaching the Temple door, she pulled it open in one swift movement, crossing again the threshold she had avoided these past decades.

BOOK OF SAMUEL, CHAPTERS 29–31

The cool quiet inside contrasted with the shouts and songs of the celebrating masses as they made their way to deposit the Horse. They would leave it a hundred paces from the Temple, Cassandra knew, the last steps to be taken in the morning, with music, food, and sacrifices. She wondered whether this was truly the end. Had Apollo allowed all this, Hector, Paris, Laocoon and so many others killed, the destruction of his own city, for vengeance?

Perhaps she could still make amends. Perhaps an apology coupled with an offer to end the feud might work; taking him on her stomach might finally get him off her back. About to put the thought into words, her mind brought her back to Hannah, praying.

She held the picture, arranged herself in the position that had worked so well for the Hebrew woman, standing, lips moving, no sound coming out. As soon as she started, she stopped in frustration—she'd offered prayers like that a thousand times. Posture could not be the whole story, because she had tried them all. Time was slipping away, the sounds of celebration reminding her of the imminent springing of whatever trap the Greeks had set.

Tears of frustration came to her eyes, running warmly down cheeks reddened by her efforts and by her fury with herself for still not being able to understand what she was being told. Sobbing, not thinking anymore, she blurted out, "Oh, Hannah, please help me! Try as I have, your lesson yet escapes me! Please tell me, what am I supposed to learn from the visions? Please, Hannah, help me save my family!"

Exactly.

The word was in and out of her head before she could react or reply, with the finality that told her she would have to figure out the rest on her own. *Exactly? What did that mean? Exactly, exactly, exactly.* She spent an hour pacing, watching the fires dwindle and die, hearing the last people leave the Horse to go home and rest for the next day. Rest, maybe that was it. Focusing on the one word she had been granted as a clue, she went to sleep, hoping to awaken with the answer.

A sound roused her before she had planned and, worse, before the solution had come to her. As it came closer, she could begin to differentiate the parts of it, hearing the cries of defenders fleeing, the joyous goading of soldiers hot in pursuit. The prickle at the back of her neck, the chills along her arm, brought back the old vision, her parents killed, she thrown to the ground and assaulted. It was time.

She moved to the altar, where the priestesses had only recently danced to attract competition for the privilege of spending a week impregnating them. She knelt before a statue of Athena—a larger version of the one in her bedroom and the only other god allowed in the Temple—eyes closed, words bubbling within but refusing to leave her mouth. Any request would be refused; it was time to accept what they would send.

The slam of the Temple's doors snapped her eyes open, turned her head to the armored man who stood there. So this was her predetermined tormentor, he who would throw her to the ground, drag her by the hair. It could easily have been worse; abstinent as she had been since before Paris' return, nothing could make her forget her standards for judging a man bedworthy.

His rippled body woke appetites she had refused to indulge since before her first dream of Hannah and the Hebrews. Seeing the punishment of Hofni and Pinhas had convinced her, fool that she was, that chastity would help her save Troy. Considering how completely she had failed, there seemed little point in continuing to forego one of life's few delights. Besides, the man's face, visible through the helmet's pulled-back visor, spoke of a kind soul hiding behind the sweat-stained, red-faced soldier who had moved to stand over her.

It became a war, the two halves of her body battling for control. The lower half wanted her to stand up and begin the mating dance, but the upper half refused to cooperate. Her mind jumped in, pleaded, *Think of all you have seen, all you have been taught. Will you throw that all away for a good-looking man?*

The reply was quick in coming. She had given the prophet side its chance, sacrificing years of ecstasy in the name of a goal. Her failure told her it was time to stop denying herself in the name of a doomed attempt to avoid Fate.

A body divided against itself cannot stand, and hers was no exception. She sat as the debate raged, content to let the Greek, or the gods, decide. He towered over her, his look making no secret of his desires or intentions, staying a second too long, or too short, on the bountiful attributes that sprang from underneath her clothing.

Chest heaving from the combined stresses of fighting his way to the Temple and his visible excitement at the prospect of taking her, he waited until his breath was closer to normal. Finally, he said, "Now I know Paris was crazy; with women like this right here at home, what would make him go searching for Helen?"

It was the sign she had sought. Thanking the gods for their guidance, she stood, moved close enough to make her intentions clear, put on the tone of voice that told a man exactly what interested her, and said, "I was his sister, so he could not sample my wares. You, on the other hand…"

He was quick on the uptake, scooping her into an embrace before she had finished. The pressure of his lips and arms was like a return home, to the days when she had known all that really mattered, the points of contact between two bodies, the rapture they could share. On the verge of losing herself for the next few hours, the sound of running in the streets gave her one last sensible thought.

Pulling free only from his lips, she whispered, "You have to force me. If they see me lie with you without a struggle, they'll assume I've been on your side all along, and will find a way to exact punishment. Throw me down here on the altar, so I can truthfully say you compelled me. I'll be safe, and then we'll have each other."

His crooked grin showed a connoisseur's appreciation of the game. "Throw you down, eh? Ajax of Locris doesn't need to rape women. We may start with rough play, but you'll be begging for more before I'm done."

Reveling in the repartee so long absent from her life, she said, "We'll see who'll be begging whom, Ajax of Locris. It has been a long time since Cassandra desired more than she was desired. As they say at the Olympics, let the games begin."

Laughing with the joy of passion realized and anticipated, he threw her down and began unbuckling his belt. Her breath caught as she watched, relishing each small moment as it came. This stage, when he had no flaws, when she had no vision of how it would end, this was the best time.

The small voice in her head still begged her to stop, tried to convince her that another vision was coming, that she had not yet understood what she was being told. It was drowned in the rush of blood to her ears and the sound of her heart's pounding. Trying to breathe while she waited for him to join her, she heard rather than saw the doors slam open, the soldier stick his head into the room.

"Agamemnon wants us all to assemble in the central square for a review of the victory and an accounting of the captured materials!"

He ran on, leaving them to pick up where they had left off. Ajax lay down next to her—she had pegged him for a jumper, was more than a little pleased at his gentleness. Desire fired her other senses one by one, but the soldier was back.

"Agamemnon says now, Ajax, and warns us that he expects to see *all* the booty, human included."

He wouldn't give in to that, would he, her chosen one? He'd stay and finish what he'd started, Agamemnon be damned, right? Grumbling, he rose, pulled her up by the hand, gave her a cloak to cover herself, and guided her out of the Temple. She made to protest, but he put a finger to her lips.

"Hush, woman! Striking as you might be, I will not make Paris' error. No woman is worth fighting Agamemnon and the entire Greek army. Pull your cape over your head; if we are lucky, we will finish our business in a little while, and then again and again over the years to come."

He pushed her before him hard enough so that others would not see how willingly she would have followed him to wherever they might find a spot to continue their coupling.

At the central square, a different man stood where she was used to seeing her father. Thoughts of her parents doused her passion, and she turned to ask some of the other captives what they knew of her family's fate. Before they could answer, the man at the front spoke, and the hush that came over the audience was obviously required of all.

His specific words were lost on her, but the power of the man was not. Looking around, seeing how his listeners yielded to him—soldiers, kings, princes, and nobles in other arenas—made her Ajax suddenly looked puny; what were his muscles compared to Agamemnon's easy command of thousands? When David would need protection from Saul, she remembered, he would turn to Achish, a powerful king, not a Goliath. Right now, the man who could protect her best was the most attractive, and in this group, it was the man addressing them all.

She pushed the cape back from her head, shrugged her cloak open, and shook out her flowing golden hair. A younger Cassandra, she knew, would have been so enticing that he would have interrupted himself to come speak with her. At her advanced age, he was able to resist the vision until after he finished speaking, laying the ground rules for how to divide the spoils. Once that was done, though, he headed straight to them.

Sensing the imminent loss of his prize, Ajax placed a protective arm on her.

"Ajax, I see you have found quite a beauty!"

The confident, commanding man from the Temple was gone, replaced by an obedient soldier. "I did, Majesty, kneeling before a statue of Athena."

"A wise choice. Have you made her yours?"

She drew in a breath, worried he would lie to keep her, a result that only an hour earlier had been painfully exciting. Compared to this new option…she took matters into her own hands. "An underling defile the daughter of Priam, king of the Greeks?! Only the king of all can have this beauty. If, that is, you think you can bear the burden of Cassandra!"

Ajax turned away in resignation, unsurprised that she would abandon him for the monarch. The Greek leader's eyes narrowed, but there was movement at the corners of his lips. "Prophetess of doom, eh? I'll take my chances for beauty such as yours; we will need to see whether the passion in your looks is reflected in the bedroom."

BOOK OF SAMUEL, CHAPTER 28

The bedroom and elsewhere, he should have said. He had certainly lived up to his half, sparking hope that the years of captivity would not be without their compensations.

Too, since the destruction of the city, there had been no fits. She'd been wrong the whole time; Apollo cared only about the destruction of Troy. That task accomplished, she would be left alone. The journey to Mycenae had been a monthlong honeymoon, the two of them lounging for hours, getting to know each other, physically and otherwise.

It would end soon enough, leaving her to learn how to be a slave/concubine. For the moment, they bounced along in the chariot, sitting closer than ordinary social comfort allowed. A month had been long enough to share life stories, hers and his, except for the one question she had hoped he would neglect to ask.

"How did you anger Apollo so much anyway?"

She'd told him of the first sighting, glossed over the rest. In fact, she'd left the Temple out of her story completely, except for when he'd asked her about Ajax. He'd said, "What about Ajax? How'd you end up with him at the Plaza?"

She'd patted Agamemnon on the hand, leaning in to give him the view and scent he loved, distracting him enough not to catch the small lie, "He found me in the Temple, grabbed me, and threw me at the altar. If the soldier hadn't caught us, he'd have violated me, put his sweaty, rough hands all over me, defiled me with his seed." She put some drama into her shudder at the thought, planted a kiss on his cheek, and snuggled into the warmth of his body. "That's for saving me from that fate."

They stayed like that until she could see the city's gates, and then he remembered his sidestepped question. "But, wait, you didn't tell me what made Apollo so mad."

She blew out a breath as he forced her to revisit the piece of the past she had thought to leave behind forever. She saw herself again at thirteen, thrilling to the first flush of womanhood, slipping away from her family for an evening at the Temple. She had not even told Helenus, afraid that word would get back, and Mother or Father would stop it. Not many were chosen to give their virginity to a god, and she was not letting any parent, no matter how well meaning, get in the way.

The walk from the palace to the Temple was short, but there was much to do when she arrived. In the outer room, where ordinary supplicants took a moment to compose themselves, she pulled off the loose, simple gown befitting a proper princess of the realm and smoothed down the seductive nightclothing she had worn underneath. At her last birthday, old Aunt Persepheus had given it to her with a wink, saying it would prove to any man she was no longer a child. *We'll see, Auntie*, she thought; *from your mouth to Zeus' ears, or, at least, Apollo's eyes.*

The dress did not need much arranging, but her hair was another matter. Removing the pins that kept in place the tight bun her parents expected, she ran her fingers quickly through the flaming halo the gossip circle had assured her would drive men wild. Did that apply to gods as well? Too late to wonder, he might step out of the room at any moment, looking for her.

Time for the final touch: reaching around her neck, she pulled up the necklaces she had worn, carefully bringing the several small canisters from their hiding places under her tunic. She applied the red, blue, and green powders where they belonged, wishing she had a better mirror than the urns in the foyer. Once she had dabbed scented water on her cheekbones, neck, and other places she hoped his nose would be traveling, she was done.

"Wait, I missed something."

Cassandra pretended to mind Agamemnon's interruption. With luck, it might consume the time until he had to take up his kingly duties, and her storytelling would be over. "What?"

"Well, I know how you met him as a six-year-old, but how did that get you to be running to his Temple to, what did you call it, 'give him your virginity'?"

"Oh, no, that started when I met him again, somewhere around halfway through my thirteenth year. Let me go back."

Cassandra practically danced down the street, enjoying her first trip to the marketplace on her own. Mother had told her only to get the fruit back to the palace in time for afternoon snack; other than that, she could linger at all the stalls and shops she wanted. At the handbag stand, she struggled with the temptation to get another; there were always new occasions for a bag, right?

"Here, Cassandra, try this one on, it will suit you perfectly."

It was him. Her breath sucked in at the sight, both out of surprise and because her hormones now let her know why muscles and beauty mattered. And he had remembered her *name*, and thought this bag would look perfect on her. Almost without thinking, she wriggled, a

90

move that called attention to the blessings the gods had bestowed upon her.

He noticed, of course he noticed; she saw his eyes flicker toward them. His touch as he put the bag to her shoulder, accidental though it must have been, tingled along her entire right side.

He said, "I see you remember me."

She looked down at the floor, unsure of how to proceed. "It was a memorable night, as I'm sure you understand."

"For me, too, although for other reasons."

Uncomprehending, she looked up. "What reasons?"

"Well, I got to meet you, of course."

Her face went red with…what? She fled the shop, ran to the fruit seller, filled her mother's list, and escaped to the safety of the palace. She might have left him physically, but he inhabited her dreams in a way he never had when she was six.

Like so many of the stories the women told, she began envisioning herself bumping into him, the innocent encounter turning into more. She would catch herself wondering what it would be like if his strong arms lifted her up like she was still a little child, carried her to the altar that dominated the front of his Temple.

Portia, her mother's attendant, had told her about doing that once with a complete stranger. In her telling, she was walking down the street one dark night, the queen having kept her late. A young widow, her physical beauty and lack of children meant she would remarry as soon as she chose.

Walking home, she was looking down at her shoes, wondering whether she needed a new pair, when she bumped into a man she had been too distracted to notice, the impact knocking her off balance. She grabbed on to him to avoid falling into the muck, a grab that turned into…well, she had made it all sound very exciting when she told the young princess about it.

Cassandra would wake in a sweat, bothered by the dreams but also worried they would never be fulfilled. After a week, the call was too strong, and she asked her mother to again let her do the shopping. Hecuba was happy to please her husband by staying out of the public eye, and to have more time for her friends.

He found her at the perfumer's, gave her what she had left behind last time. "I intended it as a gift. A beautiful bag for a remarkable young woman."

She didn't mind the blush, knowing how hard other women worked for rosy cheeks. Pleased with her grace at accepting presents, he had placed a few powders and scents in it, making sure to tell her exactly which he found most alluring.

It became a twice-weekly routine, he finding her somewhere in the marketplace, always coming up suddenly, bringing out her best color, always with some item of delight and a compliment, a joke of such cleverness it set her mind awhirl.

Agamemnon broke in again. "I don't understand. No one suspected anything?"

"What do you mean?"

"I mean a thirteen-year-old girl starts running off to the market all the time, coming back with flushed cheeks, smelling of who knows what?"

She twisted up one corner of her mouth in a wistful smile. "It's too bad you never got to meet Mother; the two

92

of you thought a lot alike. In fact, it was a conversation along those lines that made me realize I couldn't drag this on forever." To satisfy him, she turned to that part of the story.

Hecuba said, "Cassandra, I swear if I didn't know better, I'd say you have a beau."

Cassandra almost choked on the grape she was eating. "A *what*, mother?"

"A beau. You know, a young man."

"Mother, where would I meet a young man?"

"I've been wondering the same thing. You leave here for your shopping trips with a spring in your step, come back all flushed. I think I even detect the scent of perfume."

"Oh, Mother, please. I *do* enjoy the shopping, that's why I do it, and I tease the shopkeepers, and they me. It is harmless flirtation, is all, as I've seen you do many a time. And what thirteen-year-old do you know who *doesn't* apply some perfume? Am I supposed to smell like the peasants?"

He caught her next at the onion stand. As she rummaged through, looking for the ones ready for roasting, he came up behind her, as if looking over her shoulder at the produce. From the angle he had arranged, no one could see the finger that ran up her back, trailing fire with it.

She took a deep breath, squeezed her hands at her sides, and turned to face him. Mindful of appearances, he stepped back.

"Look, my mother's becoming suspicious, so we cannot meet like this anymore."

"But what shall I do without the joy of seeing my Cassandra, without her smile at my latest token of affection?"

"I've decided to give you a gift of my own; I'll meet you at the Temple tonight, but now, go, she may come to check on me at any minute."

Agamemnon appreciated the story from a man's perspective, of course. "No wonder he's a god; he's got it all, looks, technique, that slow lure, building excitement, teasing, hinting of pleasures to come."

"Which was exactly what I expected when I walked into the Temple that night."

"But?"

She shook her head, still astounded by the memory.

With one last check in the urn, Cassandra pulled open the Temple door and walked in. He was there at the bottom of the stairs, a distance of a few seconds' walk, but across a gap she only began to understand with his first words. "Ah, my latest conquest."

It was not what she had expected. "Conquest?"

"Once one has fallen for my snares, dear, there is no point in resisting."

Still more puzzled than annoyed, she said, "What do you mean?"

"Why still so far away? Come over here by the altar, where it's warmer."

Too young to stick to games and hints, she told him straight out what she wanted. "Shouldn't you come here, greet me hello with a kiss, carry me to our spot?"

He laughed. "Perhaps we ought to continue trading meaningless witticisms as well! Enough. We both know what we want, and believe me that it will be all you've dreamed of and more. But stop pretending you need me to continue wooing you; I tire of it, and the altar awaits our night of passion."

The momentum of her expectations carried her a few steps forward. She might have gone farther, until he said, "That's right. Why resist the inevitable? What woman would even want to, when they could have this?" In a moment, his clothes were off, with a flourish and a grace she found exciting in spite of the warning bells he had set off.

The body thus revealed was better than sculptors could produce. She gasped, enticed and repelled by the all-too-male flesh beckoning her. "No woman has ever resisted this body; no woman could."

A taunt too far, she didn't even have a chance to think. Her legs moved of their own accord, propelling her away from the Temple, thoughts unable to keep pace. She ran back to her room, remembering only barely in time to restore her hair and dress, threw herself into bed, and spent the night covering her sobs with her pillow.

Twenty-some years later, emotion still prevented her from finishing the story. Agamemnon reached for her hand; she squeezed his in return, turned her head into the nook between his bicep and his chest, and wept, mourning the pain, for herself and others, her stubbornness had caused. His other arm reached behind her, alternating between patting the back of her head and hugging her.

He waited until she ran down a bit to ask his next question. "Right, that's how it was for you. How did Apollo take it?"

She was spent, the words came out flat, affectless. "A week later, I had my first fit; two months after, Helenus caught fever and died."

Her life in a nutshell. One offense ruined her life and that of all those she held dear, leaving her here, a captive, bereft of family, friends, and home, adrift in the whims of Agamemnon's desires.

They arrived before he could respond, crowds of cheering citizens already lining the streets for the procession to the palace. He sat her up and slipped nimbly into the role of monarch. He stood, taking in the cheers, pointing to this or that friend or supporter, pointing at her or back at the caravans of spoils that would enrich them all.

When the chariot stopped, he beckoned for quiet, holding his arms high. "People of Mycenae! It has been a long road, and I applaud your skill at keeping our fair city—and its surroundings—prosperous in my absence. Our campaign has proven successful beyond our dreams, and it will take us time to account for all that we have. A week from now, on the plains outside the city, I invite you to join us for a full celebration, thanking the gods for their help. At that time, we hope to begin sharing our bounty. Meanwhile, for those of you who need a preview, I present Cassandra, princess of Troy!"

At the signal, she stood with bowed head, the pose he'd coached her to adopt in public. The cheer from the throng told her how well he had pegged their mood. They were anxious for evidence that the long wait for their soldiers' return would prove worthwhile. She would show that waiting one more week would reward them in full.

Fifty paces separated the chariot from the palace doors. It was only because he walked in front of her, the necessary distance between a king and his new slave, that he missed the change each step brought.

A fit, now? She almost cried out in fury. She stopped walking and closed her eyes. She would *not* let this happen, not now. She slowed her breath, counting before allowing each new one—in, two, three, four, five, out, two, three, four, and five—willing her mind to keep out the intruder.

As she cast about for ways to avoid the fit, the voice inside her, weakened from having been shouted down so many times, broke through. The pair of words she had heard the night before the Greeks jumped out of the Horse, that had never fully stopped since, again became audible in her mind. *Hannah. Exactly. Hannah. Exactly. Hannah. Exactly.*

With the difference that now she understood. Hannah, desperate enough to turn to the one God who could help her; Hannah, shorn of all hope except in the one she called Lord of Hosts. Hannah, exactly.

Fighting to keep the flailing frenzy at bay long enough to get her words out, she moved only her lips as she said, "God of Hannah, Samuel, and David, the Holy One, who they see as Creator of Heaven and Earth, as all-powerful, aid and assist me in escaping from the bond of prophecy to which Apollo has bound me. Allow me to remain silent in the face of whatever message he wishes to send me, and to build a life with Agamemnon that will at least give me peace and respite from the troubles Apollo has visited upon me. Let me live out the rest of my days in recognition that You have saved me from him, learning more about You, and announcing Your powers to the world."

The nausea did not so much ease as disperse; calm overtook her, working its way outward from the center of her body. Overwhelming all her senses, it was yet pleasant enough that not only did she not mind the loss of personal control, she knew she would be content to stay in this state forever.

Fully aware, she sensed herself on the ground, body shaking, none of which mattered, if only the Presence would stay with her. And then she saw him, an angel, a god, she knew not. So much like a man, and yet so clearly not human, he hovered above her, bathed in a light brighter than the sun's, but that caused no pain. Whatever he was, she understood immediately that he would free her of Apollo.

The vision touched her face, saying, "Cassandra, you have seen much, but missed more." His touch brought the whole story of Samuel into focus, for the first time in an ordered whole, chapter by chapter, lingering where she had failed to understand. Over and over, her teacher would correct her, "God, capital G, only *one* God!"

It was over, leaving too many questions unanswered. Who or what gave her the fits, if not a vengeful Apollo? Who was the man at the Temple? What was she supposed to do? But he was gone, a new scene playing out in her mind. Agamemnon walked into the palace, greeting his household staff, beginning to accustom himself to home. His wife's ax raining down as she split his head in two surprised Cassandra almost as much as it did its target, the bloodied man she had grown to love. Seeing herself get the same treatment shocked her, as she had not realized she was witnessing the imminent future.

The words slipped out without effort, loudly enough for all around to hear. "Clytemnestra kills, him, and then me. The abandoned wife secures her revenge! O Oenone, if only *you* had had the courage!"

The vision released her, leaving her calm and prepared. Looking around, expecting ridicule or withdrawal, she was startled to see respect and awe. She shuffled toward the palace doors, to the death Fate had meted out for her, but several men stepped in her way.

"Great Cassandra, why enter, when you know what will happen? Let us go in before you, protect you from the madwoman inside!"

She tried to think about what they said, but her mind was too confused. The Presence, the visions, the dreams, Samuel…they all blurred together. She knew she needed to focus on something, but the only option that seemed right was what her mother had said, what the sea had said, what the old judge, Eli, had said. Their motto would help her explain to these nice men why she would not accept their help. "He is God; whatever He wants will be done."

Squaring her shoulders, she walked through the palace doors.

FINAL REGRETS

I'm at a lot of deathbeds; it's an occupational hazard. All that time sitting there, you get to thinking you can categorize them. Sometimes it's a person who's been sick for a long time. There, mostly, the relatives are trying to avoid each other, afraid of letting slip how much they wish the patient would give them some peace by dying already.

Different are the sudden collapses, where the shock hasn't receded, so they barely realize what's happening. Those people are still hoping for some miracle that will bring their loved one back to them, whole as before.

Then there are the homes where money hovers over everything, either because they're all planning how to get the best share or because the widow has no idea where to get her next meal.

After all these years, I barely notice any of that. There's only so long you can see tears, breast-beating, people throwing themselves on the corpse or the floor to prove their grief, jockeying for position as chief mourner. It gets old, is all I'm saying.

I've even thought about getting out, asking for reassignment. Only thing that stops me is that occasional reminder of why I got into this side of the business to begin with. It's only every so often, when the room is limited to family or close friends, when the money stuff has been pushed aside, and the sick person is still awake, lucid, and in the mood to talk. Something about staring Death in the eye, I think, gets to these people, and, if you're lucky, you can hear the kind of straight, honest talk that's irresistible.

It especially amazes me, each time, how I enter a room thinking I can predict how it's going to play out. You know, which one's bearing a grudge, which one's trying to figure out what's in it for him, which one is just sad at the upcoming loss. That's when I'll get surprised, find out I got it backward, or sideways, or some other ways.

The day I'm thinking of, the morning had been rough. My first call was one of those really weepy scenes, which can only mean a whole bunch of guilty consciences. Turned out it was a revival of the play I like to call *Fake Guilt*. It starred, as always, the children and grandchildren who had abandoned an aging ancestor because they were too busy to cope with her infirmities.

Now that she was at Death's door, they could allow themselves to feel at fault, secure in the knowledge they would never have to actually live up to the commitments inspired by those emotions. Until the next relative got old enough, but I was pretty sure they would have pushed aside these memories by then, cleared the way for a full reenactment of the drama of neglect, guilt, tears, catharsis, and forgetting.

That gets to me more than I can tell you. The whole point of choosing end-of-life care for a career is that it's supposed to let you avoid the usual social silliness, let you see people as God intended them. When I finally got out of there, the disappointment made me pretty desperate for a satisfying death experience.

When I got to my next appointment, saw he was awake, and heard the first snippets of conversation, I relaxed. The small group surrounding him—two kids, one on each side of the bed, and a wife—bolstered my hopes. Too many people and you have to worry it's going to disintegrate into formalities, good-bye speeches aimed as much at the other people in the room as at the one leaving this world. A small family may have disadvantages, but from my admittedly narrow perspective, it gives the best shot for watching people grapple with what had been, what was about to come.

The older of the boys was on the right, farthest from the door. He had the rag ready to wipe his father's face when the periodic coughing fits racked the old man's frame. Each time he wheezed, the boy would lean over, raise his father halfway to ease the phlegm's journey out of his throat, and whisper calming phrases. Once it had passed, he would lay him back, and then return to his seat, alert for the onset of the next attack.

The widow-to-be was holding the dying man's hand, patting it, sometimes stroking the whole arm. Every few minutes, she would rewet the compress on his forehead, one of those gestures whose comfort lies in the effort rather than the effect. She spoke little, and that only to help calm her husband through a prolonged spasm. Each time it seemed like they might have reached his final moment, she would quickly whisper loving words for him to bear into the next world, a badge, proof of his impact on the world he had left.

He seemed barely able to talk, patting his son's strong arms in gratitude, and looking at his wife through liquidy eyes. After one episode, he pointed to the jug of water by the bed, took enough of a sip to wet his lips, and said to her, "It is your forgiveness I need most."

She shrugged and waved a hand, an old argument. "There is nothing to regret, let alone forgive. I joined you willingly, would do so again."

He shook his head, loath to be so lightly freed of culpability. "But to die with nothing, after so many years serving at Court! Worse, to leave you, whom I loved most, saddled with my debts!"

She moved onto the bed itself, the hand on his chest hinting at the intimacy of the years prior. "I knew you were destined for great things when we married. It has been more than enough to have been allowed to join you in the struggle that greatness requires. What comes after you are taken is God's judgment, and I will bear it with happiness, no, pride."

The twist of his lips might have been a bitter smile. "Great things, great things! Was I so foolish to have sacrificed the three of you on the altar of my dreams? To give up so much, for what? A chapter. A single chapter."

She leaned in to correct him. "A chapter for the ages, you neglect to say. You've always been blind about yourself. It was bad enough when you brought such negativity to our marriage, but to leave your sons with that as their final impression? It is beneath you; consider your words with more care."

Exhausted, he lay back on the bed, eyes closed, body motionless enough to foreshadow the permanent repose so soon to arrive. The younger son, at the foot of the bed, waited a moment, then said, head down toward the floor. "Tell us again, Papa."

His mother tried to hush him. "Your father is ill and weak; leave him alone!"

His face showed how the boy was struggling to balance his wishes against his sense of filial respect. "Mother, *you* know his life because you lived it. Considering our financial situation, grant me the only legacy I will have."

The father wanted to do it, too, you could see that, weak as he was. He sat up in bed, the cover falling away to reveal the nightshirt's thinness, emphasizing how much the disease had wasted him. The pallbearers would have no more trouble carrying this body than that of a child, and without all the pathos young death brings out.

He stifled a quick cough, held his mouth closed to head off what might have turned into a full-fledged paroxysm, and shooed away the other two, who were trying to urge him back to a fully prone position. "The boy is right; unless he—and you, my firstborn—are clear on my failures, you will not know how to avoid them for the future. I will tell the story again. I pray God gives me the strength."

He took a deep breath and paused before letting it out, head bowed, eyes closed. With the release, he said, "You must always remember how I wasted the Gift. Not many are granted it; to have let it wither within me, expressed in only one short set of Words, is a stain I will bear, I feel certain, into eternity. When you consider how to spend your time, my sons, let my deficiencies be always with you, a permanent warning resounding in your heads. Let the memory of how little I produced haunt your dreams day and night—say it to yourselves always, *a chapter, only a chapter*—let my example hold you always to the path the Lord intended. Do not let yourselves arrive at this moment, this threshold I will soon pass over, looking back at what might have been..."

There's enough tension watching someone die to put anyone on edge, but in this case, I bet the wife's knowledge of her future—the grief, the money worries, the responsibility for shepherding orphans in a tough world—were all playing with her head. She released some of it as fury.

"You're not being fair, to yourself or to me, or to what we have worked so hard for all these years! It's not as if you had the wealth and position of the others, so you could sit around all day waiting for inspiration to strike. You had a job, a family, and you've always done well by us. Why isn't that worth some satisfaction?"

His indulgent smile told all who looked that, in his mind, her judgment was clouded by her need to see the positive side of their partnership. He wasn't worried anymore about how humans would view his legacy, but about the objective evaluation of the Holy One, the literal moment of Truth. Her ministrations, sweet as they might have been, were too misted by unconditional love to soothe him. He drew her hand to his face, kissed it on the palm, and let it fall back to the bed as he continued his story.

"Your mother is right, of course; I did not grow up with social status or family money, but that only adds to my sense of guilt over the difficulties I have caused you. God cares about what we accomplish, not about how many obstacles we had to overcome."

The older one, it seemed, was his mother's child. "But Pa, how can you say you left us with nothing? Surely your years of service to His Majesty—"

His eyes squeezed shut, the mention of his employer paining him. "Please. The king relied on me for advice and assistance, it is true, but his memory does not extend much beyond the day he is currently living. Aside from which, before I became ill, he called me in, wanted to know why he isn't doing better financially, if I'm so righteous."

All three moved to protest, but he stopped them with a raised hand. "I know, I know, but he said that when Our Father Jacob worked for Laban, the whole household was blessed, and surely he is no worse than Laban!" He shook his head. "Had I only realized the cost of working for him, I would have scrambled to survive elsewhere and otherwise."

The intensity on the younger son's face as he watched his father reminded me of nothing so much as when I had seen others attempt to memorize every nuance of what was happening. He said, "Elsewhere and otherwise?"

The dying man sucked in a sharp breath, clamped his mouth shut for a minute more, and nodded as he began to speak. "I know what you're thinking, that I had limited options, not having ancestral land. But to join a Palace as infested with evil as that one, I should have known better, especially knowing Edom as I do...I mean, that was a perfect example of the enticements of evil, where *their* forefather found evil even growing up in a house infused through and through with good..." he trailed off, shaking his head, and picked up the thread. "Protecting myself was all I could do. You will, thank God, never know this insecurity, but with my late start at serious study, I could not tell when everyone else was wrong, and when it was just my ignorance revealing itself. For years, I ran to Master Elijah with the silliest questions. It took longer for me to absorb the truth that people could violate the most basic commandments and still be *sure* they were right."

His wife opened her mouth for her ritual protestation, but the older son stepped in. "Pardon me, Mother, but might I be allowed? Father, why do you minimize your successes so? Surely, the Lord chose you for that message, and you can take satisfaction in having fulfilled your task. I say honestly, Father, I only hope that when my time comes, I will have half the greatness I see in you."

The admiration, freely given, forced him to stop for a moment, but only for that long. "Don't you see, though? For all His Majesty's flaws, he had a point. Were I truly righteous, the Lord surely would not have withheld his blessings from the Palace. None of us would say His Majesty was worse than Laban, would we?" His look was more a warning than a question.

Satisfied, he tried to continue, but his mouth had gone dry. He reached for the jug again, but the repeated wettings of the compress had exhausted it. He inverted it over his mouth, hoping for a last drop, then gave it to his wife. "Dear, would you mind?

The younger son stood, saying, "Here, Ma, let me do it," but she shook her head and left. As soon as she was out of earshot, he sat his son down with a hand motion, and said, "Your mother knows what I wanted to tell you, and she cannot stand to be here for it. You have always been respectful boys, and I thank you for that. It is only because of that that I have been able to avoid telling you of my greatest shame, the reason I know God denied me more of His Word.

"We have always pretended, in this family, that I know Edom so well because I chose to study them, to learn about our greatest enemy as an academic adventure. True as that might be, it is not the whole of it. The same goes for my late arrival at the study of God's Word. The whole truth is that I was not born of Israel, but...of Edom."

The two brothers looked at each other, I would have thought in surprise; from my experience, hearing your father's from a different nation, let alone one of the most hated ones around, would rock the kids. The look between them went on long enough, though, that I realized they were trying to figure out which of them would answer. The older one began. "Father, we know."

His eyes, which he had closed as much to avoid seeing their hurt faces as to recoup some strength, flew open. "You knew?"

"Of course. Do you think the children of the other retainers would forego a chance to tease us for our lineage?"

His artlessness dawned on him only as he heard himself articulate his thoughts. "But what about the prohibition against deriding the convert and his descendants?"

The younger one snorted. "Father, in a Palace led by His Majesty, did you consider the possibility that this commandment, like the others, might fall by the wayside?"

"But then, why did you not say anything?"

"We spoke to Mother, and she said you would tell us in your own time and way. She said you were a very important man, and that your work would suffer if you thought we were burdened by your choices."

A tear formed at each of his eyes. "Another mark on my record. I always regretted the time I took from you to go out to the caves, to bring food and drink to the fugitive prophets. But what could I do, watch Her Majesty snuff out their light, steal the Word from our midst? And now, you are left to bear the debts I accumulated…" Each tear made its way down a cheek, meeting again at the mouth. He lapped at the salty taste, as if the bitterness was an introduction to the afterlife he expected.

The older one began, but the younger one stopped him. Rising from the foot of the bed, he made his way around to the side left vacant by his mother. Instead of sitting on the chair, he lowered himself onto the edge of his father's bed, put his arm behind his father's back, and raised the dying man to a sitting position, supporting his father's emaciated frame with the ease of those too young to realize that their strength will one day be lost.

Moving his shoulder to support his father's head, he said, "Father, listen, please! You are being too hard on yourself, for no reason. Think of the esteem in which Elijah held you. He once said to us that he respected many of his disciples, but he loved you. How many of the children who were teasing us knew of the exalted task we had the privilege to share, and that all we had to do to was not complain when you left home? How many children had the privilege of a father who found his way to God coming from the most despised nation on Earth?"

The older brother was more literal. "None, Papa, that's how many. Whatever has been, whatever will be, worrying yourself on our account is a waste of time and effort. When you are judged, nothing of what has happened in our lives will be counted as anything but a merit. So please, Father, lie back, and calm yourself." With those words, the younger son slid him back onto the soft blankets they had placed beneath his head, moving a centimeter at a time, intent on not dropping the weakened man.

The wife reentered, smiling with a cheeriness she could not possibly have felt. It was she, I knew, who would have to fend off the creditors after he died, she who would have to save her sons from being snapped up by the many bad influences that would vie for their attention. She placed the refilled jug to her husband's lips, the smile never faltering.

He wasn't buying it. "You heard what the boys said, I assume."

She nodded. "Indeed I did. They are good boys, and I thank you for giving them to me. They will be my only comfort when…"

The pain wrinkled his face. "Comfort, yes, protection, no. What was I thinking, mortgaging my family's future for the safety of others?"

She rewet the compress, put it on his forehead, and ran her damp hand over the rest of his face, cooling and stroking at the same time. It was a gesture of such love and intimacy, I had to turn away.

Her words reached me. "Whatever you have done, we have done. It was admiration, not desperation, that led me to marry a man who chose to join our people. To come from a rabble that does not even pass their monarchy by legacy, do not even have a language of their own—"

"Please, dear, mocking my past isn't helping."

Some heat crept into her voice. "Well, it should be. It should give you confidence in how God will see you, knowing where you came from and where you got to. How many Edomites even recognize God, let alone become one of His prophets?"

The older son stepped a toe into the argument. "If I may add, Mother, not just any prophet, but a contributor to the permanent record."

His head moved back and forth with remarkable energy for one whose time was fast approaching, as he said, "No, no, no, you're getting carried away with seeing the good side. Which neglects the truth, that, if I could do what I did, do you not realize how much *more* I could have done? Think of all the others who knew what I was doing out at the caves, who could have earned a reward by reporting me to the king, and said nothing. A better man, I guarantee you, would have built on that, gotten them involved somehow, used that as an opening to bring them back to God.

"Or all those nights, years, I spent striving to get more prophecies. What if I had accepted the Judgment that that phase of my life was done, and had put my energies into more productive activities? Or what if, instead of allowing myself to enjoy the comforts of the Palace, I had taken the three of you to a remote place, where my prophecy might have flowered more? To have brought only a drop from the Well when I might have slaked the people's thirst for the Lord...Ah, the shame!"

"But, Father," the older one was trying again, "if Master Elijah didn't succeed, why do you blame yourself? Perhaps you were not fated for success, as he was not."

A note of impatience crept into his reaction, the first I had seen. "Agghhh, don't you see? Master Elijah was a different being; he was not *meant* to be of the people, to work from within. He was the living embodiment of service of God, of dedication to Truth. If he had succeeded, it would have been on a national scale; his failure reflects the people's lacks, not his own. The Lord did not expect that of me, a man of such limitations. But my failures, don't you see, were all mine."

I almost stepped in, but it wasn't quite time. This was for the family to work out; my job would come soon enough. The wife and older son were silenced, unhappy, frustrated. They knew there had to be a way to ease his passage to his eternal rest, but could not find it. Stubborn insistence that you have run a bad race is hard to combat, particularly as the person is gasping for his last several hundred breaths.

The younger son would not yet admit defeat, still shared his father's belief that the right words could always achieve the desired result. He was clearly weighing those now, unsure how much time he had left to move his father from self-flagellation to contentment.

Finally, he began. "Father, perhaps Mother and Joshaphat are unable to sympathize, but I can. Aside from gratitude for the many gifts you have given me, I also share your insistence on seeing what might have been, of being aware of how I have failed in my quest for perfection.

"I have listened to your story, have understood what upsets you about it, and yet, I think you have neglected the fullest picture. Perhaps you are right in all you say; I will not contradict you. Perhaps a different person would not only have converted from Edom, not only prophesied their doom, but would have inspired change in them as well, helped them avoid the future he had seen. Perhaps a different person would not only have resisted the evil of the House of Ahav, but would have brought them to the good. Perhaps a different person might not only have saved the prophets from Her Majesty Queen Jezebel, but done so without taking loans at interest that will burden his survivors."

He paused, the look on his face telling me he knew he had hooked his father, that letting the silence hover would keep the dying man wondering where he could possibly be going by conceding so much. After the tension had stretched to its fullest, he continued. "But Father, recognizing what might have been does not negate the greatness that was. Think of this. You have always told us of how far you fell from your teacher, Elijah, from your peers, Jonah, Micah, and Elisha. But, Father, which of them can say he accomplished all he was meant to? Jonah, who fled from his assigned task? Elijah and Elisha, who have not bothered to write up even a chapter of their experiences? And, not to toot your sons' horns, which of them left children dedicated to building on the foundation he laid in his life?"

The man on the bed was beginning to fade, the thread of the conversation getting away from him. At the last name, he gripped his wife's arm, and repeated it. "Elisha, Elisha!"

She thought he was delirious, as did I, and patted the hand gently. "Yes, dear, Elisha; you had some good times together."

"No, no. Elisha! He will help, if you have trouble. Whatever it is; if His Majesty hounds you, or our creditors, if they want to take the house, or the boys; tell me you will remember—when times get unbearable, go to Elisha, and he will see you through!"

He was done; they could see it, I could see it, and I got myself ready. The two boys lapsed into silence, respecting their father's final moments, the tears beginning to flow.

The man's lips were still moving, rejecting all his family's attempts. "One chapter, and to the Edomites yet! Ah, the shame!"

It was time. I stepped forward, allowing him now to see me, recognizing the look of fear. I took pleasure that this day, I had the good fortune of ratifying his younger son's sentiments. "No, friend Obadiah, you have me wrong. I come to bring you to the Throne, to reside there among the Lord's beloved." He moved to protest as he had with his family, but I did not have to listen. "Obadiah, you have forgotten our Lord's motto: whether a lot or a little, as long as you put your heart fully toward His service. It is how well you try, not how much you accomplish."

And with that, the worry eased from his face, a smile playing at his lips. I let it linger there long enough for the family to see, to know he had found the peace of mind they had worked so hard to give him. And then I took his soul, escorting it Above, reminded why I asked the Lord for this assignment all that time ago.

PROPHET SEEKS AGENT

So this guy comes into my office, I want to say all breezy-like, because the way my door works there's *always* a breeze when someone walks in, 'cept *he* gets there and nothing, no wind at all. Which got my attention, ya know? So when I look up, my hand's already reaching for my right pouch, where I keep my dagger, in case there's any trouble.

It wasn't that I felt threatned—I can handle myself okay, been around the block a few times—but somethin' about him, his height, maybe, the way he carried himself, this attitude he gave off, said he wasn't a guy who got intimidated. Which for me usually means he's planning on doing the intimidating.

I wasn't too happy when he nods his head at my right side and says, "That won't be necessary," as if he had read my mind, since I'm pretty sure I got my hand in there 'fore he could've seen. But I trained myself to handle all kinda situations, so I put it away, ask him how can I help, and he tells me his name, says he's looking for better spread for his word, get it out there more. Only I'm thinking he said Word.

I shoulda done like my first thought, told him we're not a match, that I focus on storytellers, not prophets. But he had this aura, like getting him to take my no would be a whole lot harder unless I had looked through the stuff. And it wasn't that he was big and built; I deal with lots of guys taller, and it ain't muscle that wins fights, it's what you do with 'em.

Nah, it was more like this steady calm, like how even his hair—which had some gray; I was surprised 'cause the face had so few wrinkles—sat on his head, every one in place, or the way his back stayed straight. Most people sitting like that, you think they've got a stick up their you-know-what. For him, it seemed natural, like that happened to be the way he liked to sit.

I thought about invitin' him to come back once he made a formal appointment, but then I figure, what the hell, it's probly easier to get it over with now, so I ask if he's brought any samples. He gives me a few scrolls, and the writing's fine, nothin' great, but I could work with it if I had to. But—here's the part that's gonna blow your sandals off—he tells his readers he's married Gomer, Divlayim's daughter.

It took all of my control not to whistle at that, because I've taken a ride on that caboose, and, 'spensive as it was, it was more than worth it. And he's *married* her, knowing she might still be tricking!

But it was worse, 'cause he writes about their kids, and he's not even sure they're his, *and* he saddles them with these names, linked to his predictions, you know? I don't care *who* he thinks he is, you don't bring business home, is what I say.

I know, I know, you're gonna tell me the whole prophet thing makes it different, that people'll forgive a lot that would look out of line coming from you or me, but my experience? There's serious limits to that, and marrying a prost...a lady like that, ain't gonna go over big when you're trying to point up other people's flaws and failings. He didn't even make her get outta the profession, for crying out loud!!!

Anyway, I try to express my concerns to my prospective client—yeah, yeah, I can talk good when I gotta, say things like *raise his comfort level with his representation*—but

118

he's not worried. He tells me to move on to the next section, where it'll become clearer. So I go on, figuring he'll explain or apologize for his weakness for ladies of, how should I put it, dubious reputation?

But no, he turns it into a metaphor, his messed-up-marriage-as-symbol-for-the-people's-relationship-with-God. Now look, I got no problem with the prophet gig, lots o guys have used it and gotten good word of mouth and good sales, but he's not showing the judgment he needs. Who's he to complain about how the people are betraying God, when he don't care so much about faithfulness, living with a woman like *that*?

I mean, if he's gonna get people to listen to him rail against them, whether it's as individuals, communities, or a whole country, he's gotta take care of things at home first, is what I say. Because his wife is one piece of work. You know, I wonder if she *is* still working, 'cause I might spring for another roll, if you know what I'm saying.

But I digress. So I read through, and it's the usual, God's going to bring troubles, we won't find any allies, won't have any money. Course, you know how a guy like me, with my friends, is going to react to the whole God with a capital "G" thing, especially paired with the *your money problems are because of your religious failings* tirade. Way I see it, long as I've given this god his due, ain't none of his business how many other bases I'm covering; the more gods I keep happy, the safer I should be.

Least that's how I figure it, so I'm thinking I can stop here, tell him there's no public for that message—and if there is, I'm not the one to find them—and get on with my day. I'm a little annoyed at how much he's got me thinking 'bout what to say to him, 'cause how often do I need more'n a minute before rejecting a client?

But I'm trying to compose myself to let him down gentle, when the next little section catches my eye. Turns out he married *another* woman at God's command—maybe this deity's more fun than I been giving him credit for—but get this, he had to find one whose husband kicked her out for cheating! And he pays more than she's worth, which don't seem too smart to me; the whole point of a bargain is the price, no? And *then* tells her they're not gonna consummate their relationship, with each other *or anyone else,* for a long time!

Marrying Man's extremes were starting to make me nervous, accepting one woman's being a little loose, and then going all the way to abstinence. As an agent, I'm thinking of my readers, and they're gonna be confused by this guy, whether he's a swordsman, as we might say, or a prude. You got to make your character clear to the readers, one of the first rules of writing.

So I start explaining what he's doing wrong and, just to be a little helpful, I make some suggestions, like that he tone it down a little, put in some of the kinds of positive prophecies where God'll take care of us, give us a good life. Maybe once he's established some cred, got a following, he can slip in the complaints.

He's listening, I can see that, but it's weird, 'cause his eyes, did I tell you about them? Well, he's got the schnozz we all do, so the eyes're far apart, but in his case they're also set pretty deep in his face. You'd think that would make them less noticeable, especially with that large mouth and thick lips, always twisted in a half smile.

Yet the eyes, they're so full of…I can't put my finger on it, but they grab your attention away from everything else. That first time, I didn't even notice the scar, the one that starts in the middle of the right ear and runs down to almost his jugular, like from a knife fight gone too far, until he starts getting angry at what I'm saying.

He's listening to me use my best vocabulary and diction, you know the whole *while your work seems interesting,*

I believe it does not fit my current profile of authors, but the scar starts to pulse, like the blood's about to boil out of it, and the eyes start to burn, and I'm wondering maybe I do need my dagger. But then he breathes twice—deep, like four, five seconds a breath—and his eyes start looking out instead of at me, and his good ear's cocked, like it's listenin' to sounds I can't hear.

I finish, and he sits, the fire in his eyes receding, the beat in the scar slowing down, still listening to that distant music. A minute goes by, and I'm starting to wonder how long I'm supposed to wait, thinking of ways to get him out of my office, when he says, "Thanks for your time; I'll be back," and goes.

I was glad, too, 'cause he gave me the spooks. I mean, I've seen a lot of these prophet types, and they can all go into pretty convincing trances, which is fine, and I give my donations, and whatever. But Distant-Eyes was different, didn't seem the type to be bought off with a shekel or two. So when he walked out the door, I was fine with bidding him good riddance.

Why'm I tellin' you all this? Calm down, I'm getting there. All right, all right, no need to get huffy; we can handle this without calling in Gigantor. I'm telling you all this because I got fifty copies of his book here, it's a short read, just fourteen chapters. I thought if you took a few— on consignment, no risk to you—you could sell them, like when customers ask you what's new, what's hot. With a little pushing, I figure, you could make a little money.

How is it I'm representing him? At's what I was trying to tell you, gimme a minute, what else you got doing? Store seems pretty empty today anyway. Okay, fine, go help the old lady, I'll wait here by these sacks.

Ready? Right, so he leaves that first time, but a week later, he's back. I get him seated, start reading, but my own attitude's shifting. Bug me one time, you're a kook, but come another time—and with new material—you're a pesky kook. So I read the new stuff, and it's pretty much more of the same, you know, anger and, um, vitriol, I guess you'd say, about corruption, abandoning God, mistreating other people, lying, who knows what.

I'm preparing my rejection as I skim, because his A for tenacity is offset by his F for advice-taking, 'cause there's nothing positive here at all, meaning I couldn't help him much even if I wanted to, you know? I mean, you know how it is out there; if you're not willing to give the people what they want, there's nothing your agent can do for you.

Things might have ended there, but a messenger arrives. Did I ever show you the two doors in my office? Well, aside from the usual one, where Prophet Man and other ordinary clients come in, I've got one hidden behind that deerskin, for matters that need my "urgent-but-discreet" attention, if you catch my drift, and that's where he comes, sent by Jonathan.

On the q.t., I can tell you that Jon's been a great client from even before he got to be High Priest. I love him too 'cause he's one of the few people I know who appreciates my discretion. His stuff's usually routine—fix a contract, get a promotion for a friend, shepherd court cases away from Temple liability, stuff like that—but the last piece I'd done for him had gone awry, so I had to take this call.

I'm not a wet work kinda guy, which is why I was worried about how he would react to this. It's not that I got any problem with it; you know me, I'm happy to set you up with somebody if that's what you need. But I picked my niche a long time ago, and it's the on-the-line-between-respectable-and-not. It's a positioning thing, representing certain books and authors means drawing lines.

So when the High Priest asked me to "strongly caution" this guy, I only meant to warn him to keep up with his payments. But the poor slob's desperate 'cause the vig on his loan is killing him and his kids ain't got what to eat, so he comes at me with an axe. I only meant to disarm him, I swear, 'cept when I hit him, the bastard's nose shoots up into his brain, and he up and dies on me.

Point is, prophet in my office or no, I got to make sure the High Priest's not mad for getting possibly linked to that kind of thing. I'm trying to get away subtle, not call attention to the messenger behind the other door, so I use my best polite voice to ask him to wait a moment while I deal with an urgent matter.

Ramrod Back's sitting on the edge of his seat doing his listening thing, half smile on his face. And *he* says, calm, relaxed, but with an edge, like the whole business bothers him, "Need to explain to your employers how it came about that you killed a father of two young children over a few shekels?"

My jaw must have dropped a little, because he nodded as he went on, saying, "Oh, yes, the Lord sees and knows all," or some such.

Which ticked me off, because I'd been pretty sure I disposed of the whole matter with maximum secrecy. But I control myself, give some kind of whatdoyoucallit?—an answer that doesn't say anything, yeah, noncommittal—and go. I tell the messenger the story, spin it right, tell him I got it covered so even the family don't know the truth. I leave out Scar-Throat sitting in the other part of the office, but I'm hoping he's too busy bearing the Word to be distracted by one minor incident.

Jonathan's guy totally buys it, waves off the small glitch, raves about how pleased they are with my services, blah, blah, blah, and I'm relaxing, enjoying how easy it is to keep them happy. As I'm nodding and smiling, I'm thinking how maybe if the client in the other part of the office learned to do some of that, he wouldn't need someone like me to peddle his stuff in the first place!!!

The messenger's next words catch me so off guard, I take a moment to realize he's "extended the High Priest's invitation to dinner." That night! You ever gotten one of those? Well, for me, it's a real step up. Publishing's a rough business—we all know that—we're all killing each other for market share, so we understand that some people have to act differently than others.

But the priests have always looked down on me, like what I do is a little degrading. Sure, they'll *hire* me, but I'd always gotten the feeling they were leery of mixing business with pleasure, least with me. Socializing was for their snooty friends, not the lugs they deal with all day. So this invite's a big deal, and I come back to the office smiling, in the middle of daydreaming about moving up in the world.

I walk in ready to pick up where we'd left off, but he's got other plans. First thing, he says, "Sure, I'd love to go to his house for dinner; what time should I get you?"

He knows how to take the bloom off the rose, I'll tell ya. I tried setting him straight, telling him I couldn't bring extra people, begging him to let me have this one night. I even offered to take him on as a client if he'd promise not to show.

But he's set, and I figure if he knows I got invited, he could get there on his own, which would be worse. Least if he comes with me, he might restrain himself a bit. Figuring it's the best of the bad options, I set a time.

What? I'm trying, I promise, but unless you hear the whole thing, you ain't gonna understand how I got to be here peddling his book, and without that, I bet you won't give it the consideration it deserves. I promise you, five minutes, I'm done and outta here.

And don't be heavin' no sighs at me neither, I knew you before you were Mr. High-and-Mighty, and I'm pretty sure I could send you back there if I put my mind to it, know what I mean? What's that, a little wine? Yes, thanks, that'd be great.

He picks me up, me having washed my face and hands, all clean, ready to go and take my career to the next level, which will require two steps: wowing the guests at Jonathan's house, and freeing myself of my dinner date. To lay the groundwork, I ask him why he even wants to go. He's this prophet or whatever, thinks it's the corruption of these kinds of people that's hurting the nation, then why's he want to have dinner with them?

He gives me that smile, which starts to grow on you, especially since this time I could have sworn there was some humor in it, and says, "You'll see," and shuts up. I try again. Usually, asking a guy like him what made him want to be a prophet gets you a monologue longer than you ever thought you'd hear, but he looks at me funny, and says, "I don't think anybody *wants* to be a prophet; we are called."

I didn't know what that meant, because…right, exactly, all the ones I see are desperate to get prophecies; they're meditating, purifying, floggin' themselves, or whatever. When I ask him, he shoots air out his nose, and says, "No, I mean the real ones, where God sends the Word, to deliver to whoever *He* wants. You think that's pleasant? You think I wanted to saddle my children with names like Jezreel, No Comfort, and Not My Nation? I am what I am because the Lord determined it would be so. As you'll see at dinner tonight."

We walk on, me thinking hard. Rare as it is, I know when someone has leveled with me, and he had rocked me a bit. I'd *read* about people who pursue their goal at great personal cost, but I never believed they existed. I was also worrying over his last words, which weren't good news. I needed that dinner to go smooth, otherwise… well, let's get to otherwise.

I start trying to persuade him that I could help him more if the night went well, but we're already there, and Jonathan's on his doorstep greeting people. The High Priest gives me a big smile, although no handshake or hug, no physical contact, you know those priests and their contamination rules.

Then he sees the guy walking next to me, and his face shuts down. His "You brought him?" look don't carry good news for me, so I say, real quick, "No, he overheard and came on his own."

You don't get to be High Priest by being a shrinking violet, and I can see he's thinking of saying something to my companion, even though etiquette won't let him send him away without food once he came. My prophet's not one to back down neither, which I kinda admired, that he'd stare down the High Priest at his own house, but the shouting match that's brewing wouldn't do me any good, so I move between them and up close to Jon. He steps back to avoid physical contact, like I knew he would, and me and my guy slip into the house.

Once the fifteen of us are around the table, some idiot asks him what he does. I'm about to interrupt, steer us to a discussion of publishing, but those eyes start burning, and he lets loose. New complaints I never saw in the scrolls, about how the priests are leading the people to destruction, and the prophets too.

The priests, for God's sake! He couldn't take on somebody else that one night, when we're sitting at a priest's table, and some of the guests are eating priest-tithe? One thing I'll tell you, he don't lack for *cojones*.

And he goes on and on, that liberal social justice crap these dreamy types always harp on, how we need to be kinder to the poor and hungry, how bad the corruption in the higher circles is, stealing, killing, who knows.

As he's sending my career down the tubes, I'm fuming. It would be one thing if he took me down for an idea I could relate to, but here, it's like he doesn't realize that you've got to keep a Temple going somehow, like he doesn't know you've got to cut a corner here or there, break some eggs to make a cake.

I'm about to step in, set him straight, calm everybody down, but the host has already had enough. He storms away, some kind of signal to the others. He couldn't be involved in any fighting himself; word would get out and, besides, he'd have to spend a day away from the Temple.

The other guests don't got the same scruples, and things get pretty wild. Even more wild is how the whole way through—the shouting, the fighting, the throwing stuff—my guy's cool. He ducks when he needs to, but mostly stands there, this calm, satisfied look on his face, like he's done his job, the rest is out of his hands. And somebody was watching over him, because not much does happen to us. Oh, sure, a stray punch broke my nose as I stood back-to-back with him, but that's no big deal.

Back-to-back? Surprised the devil out of me, too, but not him, like he knew I couldn't resist a guy so crazy as to go to the High Priest's *house* to speak to his closest friends about how corrupt they all are; pure lunacy like that, it's like a precious natural resource, and you know what a sucker for nature I am.

I think someone hit him once or twice in the stomach, but he gave pretty good, too, and the whole time, he's still talking! Not real loud, but you could hear him through all the noise, promising destruction, exile, and death, and like he's just relaying a message. To stay on point like that even in the middle of a brawl...kudos to him, you know?

By the time it's all over, us having been ushered from the premises not so gently, my career on, let's say long-term hold, because no way is anyone going to believe I wasn't in this with him, and, like I said before, my business depends on how much people can trust me, and when word gets out...

Anyway, so I got nothing to lose, figure I can talk straight, no need to worry about burning bridges. I start with the pretty obvious idea that he might try working within the system instead of standing on the side criticizing, that he could have tried cultivating these people, you know, getting to know them, what makes them tick, finding positive, friendly ways to get them to change a little. Step by step'd work a whole lot better than his take-no-prisoners approach.

Or, if not that, he could try weaning the people from how much they resent the prophets by showing them he's got a side other than always frickin' telling them what they're doing wrong.

He listens, eyes focused on me for once, which wasn't as good as it sounds because the power in them was hard to take. When he answers this time, it's gentler; he says, "But don't you see the love in His persistence? He sends me, Amos, Micah, Isaiah! Don't you understand that if God *wanted* to punish, it would've happened a long time ago, that He delays because He's hoping for change?"

Frustrated, I say, "Well, maybe we're not good enough; did you ever think of that? Maybe we need a few extra gods to feel secure. Maybe we need a little interest on loans to support a Temple and avoid starvation. And maybe…"

He doesn't let me finish, coming back with "Why are you all so sure you can't do it His way? Have you tried? Think of the Fathers! Remember Jacob, worked fourteen years for his goals? If we tried harder to live up to their examples, you can't imagine where we could get!"

And then—and I'm not gonna get this right because I'm only an agent, not a writer—but as he's talking, he stops looking at me, his eyes are completely gone, I don't know where, and all of a sudden his words aren't his, he's taking dictation. And these words, they're beautiful like I never heard, like every one's poetry.

At the time, I only caught parts of it, how we should return—"Return, O Israel" that was the opening, pretty strong, huh?—but it was smooth like linen, beautiful like butter, like there's no tomorrow. And it was all that positive stuff I was talking about, God taking us back, putting aside our sins, healing us. I couldn't tear my eyes away.

I don't know when I had started realizing this was a guy I had to help, but that moment clinched it. Once you've seen that, believe me, it don't matter the cost, you gotta do what you can. Least, I do; turns out I got an idealistic side I didn't know about.

Point is, I agreed to take him on. He didn't let me touch content, but we worked together on the order. I figure lead with the Gomer stuff, sex sells, right? And then put that last bit at the end, because that's the kind of speech that'll build up buzz; people might even decide to read it aloud on some important occasion, and others'll go through the rest of the scroll to get to it, that's how moving it is. Here, I got it open, see?

That was, what, five months ago? And even though I only was hoping to get the Word out there, it's been rough, because every store I walk into, they all want to know if they're the first, then they turn me down. I didn't want to impose on our personal relationship too much, but I'm getting to the end of my rope, and thinking maybe I need to call in one of those markers; remember that Cushite deal? Yeah, yeah, that was great.

Oh, sure, I understand, and I'm not suggesting I'm gonna pressure you too much. I haven't had a job since the night of that dinner, so it's not like I've got a lot of power right now. Look, let me leave you a copy, you can work your way through it, and I can stop in a few days from now for a decision. Absolutely. Sure, sure, I know where you're coming from. No, no, thanks for *your* time. Yeah, great. Regards to the wife, and all that, and I'll see you in a couple of days.

What's that? Nah, my business is pretty much gone anyway. Worst case, I lose my investment and go off to my family's farm up north, get back to the land and all that. Best case? You sell out, other guys sign up, we get a few thousand copies out there, I get a new start, and seventy years from now, maybe a couple of people remember my prophet.

What's that? Yeah, I thought of that, but I don't dare think that way. People knowing the name of Hosea son of Beeri in three thousand years? Just not gonna happen.

DRAFT REPORT OF THE SHEVNA COMMISSION ON THE EXECUTION OF ISAIAH, SON OF AMOTZ

CAUTION: The following is *only* a draft. Any conclusions of fact or judgments of propriety are tentative. We circulate this draft primarily to allow those implicated a chance to respond, comment, or criticize. It should be considered classified, access limited to those who appeared before this Commission or are mentioned by name.

I. Mandate of the Commission: Administering the death penalty obligates reflection and soul-searching. In most cases, that extends only to the courts and the most involved witnesses, but it becomes incumbent on all of us when the executed sinner was a member of the royal family and a prophet to the nation.

We express our deep gratitude to His Majesty, the Anointed One of God, King Menasseh, for privileging us to investigate this matter. His empowering the Commission to examine the circumstances leading up to the recent death of Isaiah, son of Amotz—known as the Prophet Isaiah—invested us with a most sacred task. It was His Majesty's hope, and ours, that this report will provide avenues of growth for all Israelites.

We thank His Majesty for granting the Chair, Shevna the Scribe, such broad authority of subpoena and secrecy. Only these powers allowed us to find the truths contained here—and soon to publish them—without fear of retribution or reprisal. For the same reasons, the identities of Commission members are to be kept unknown until thirty years from the publication of this report.

To assure the public that these conclusions come from qualified voices, we note that the choice of members was brought to five tribal leaders for advice and consent. Thirty years hence, when the seal will be broken on the supporting materials we have buried under the Great Court, all Israelites will be able to review our procedures and assure themselves (we hope) that we have handled our responsibilities in a manner befitting those invested with the public trust.

His Majesty charged the Commission in three areas: the precipitating events, with special attention to whether and how this outcome might have been avoided; the trial and execution itself; and enunciating strategies to avert such tragedies in the future.

Early meetings produced agreement that the task as defined could take up many lifetimes. For only one example, were we to attempt to fully discuss a forty-year prophetic career, we would necessarily either lose ourselves in meaningless generalities or become bogged down in details, the interpretation of this or that phrase, and other distractions. We sought to produce a report short enough for all members of our people to attend to from start to finish, yet insightful enough to teach lessons of value.

To achieve that middle path, we decided, again unanimously, to focus on the main actors in these events. A consensus developed that evaluating the roles of His Majesty, the High Priest Hilkiyah, and the Prophet, would come as close as feasible to fulfilling His Majesty's mandate. That decision shaped the three questions that guide this report:

1) Was the indictment properly handled? When a person is removed from power, we cannot ignore the possibility that interpersonal conflicts, jealousies, or other improper motives played a role. To that end, the Commission spent much time investigating the background, to see whether there was probable cause to initiate the proceedings.

2) Did the preparations for the trial and its actual conduct follow established procedures? Was the defense allowed sufficient time for rebuttal or refutation? Was there a "rush to judgment," as it were?

3) In the process of convicting and executing the Prophet, were his rights—and the sanctity of the act—secured at all points?

In hundreds of hours of interviews, the Commission has found remarkable consistency of voice among the participants. We hope that unity means we have come to accurate conclusions, although only God can fully protect from errors.

A last technical point: each occurrence chronicled here was verified by at least two witnesses. We have sometimes recorded speculation, but only when two people expressed the same view independently of each other.

II. Precipitating Events: The idea of bringing the Prophet to trial first came up at a weekly briefing. These meetings, unknown to the general public, offer Our Master the High Priest a chance to update His Majesty on rates of offerings and tithes, foot traffic at the Temple, and other pressing aspects of his administration. Once the facts have been reported, the High Priest tends to raise an idea for Palace-Temple cooperation. Witnesses confirmed that this part of the briefing generally focuses on areas where the public might be effectively moved to the next stage in its service of God.

At the meeting in question, Our Master Hilkiyah broached the question of improving gift-giving to Levites. The Levites' tithe did not inspire the same care among the people, and the tribe was suffering from intractable poverty.

Readers may remember that a starving Levite had collapsed and died the week before, forcing the crisis into the public consciousness. High Priest Hilkiyah asked His Majesty to generate ideas on how to avoid a recurrence.

Long-standing custom required these sessions, but the king made little secret of how burdensome he found them. His advisers have told us how frequently he complained about the time wasted on these chats, since all the ideas generated withered for lack of implementation.

That conversation ran down, normally the end of the meeting. This day, though, the High Priest cleared his throat and fussed with the place on his tunic where his breastplate would have sat had he been on the Temple grounds. "Um, Majesty, actually there was one more matter."

His Majesty's face clouded over, but his voice came out fully composed, as always. "Yes, Master High Priest, how else can We assist you?"

Hilkiyah spoke in the measured, deliberate style the populace so adores. "What I suggest is difficult, I know, particularly because of the blood ties between His Majesty and the Prophet..."

His Majesty's face twisted at the reference. "We have had no contact with Our grandfather beyond what any occupant of this Throne would; soon after Father Majesty King Hezekiah produced an heir, they had a falling-out."

Hilkiyah's eyebrow rose. "Falling-out?"

The ruler glanced at the hourglass on the window. "We assume you know of the Prophet's role in the defeat of Sanheriv?"

Hilkiyah nodded, he having been the one to suggest that the Temple hold an annual dinner commemorating the Late Majesty Hezekiah's victory over the king of Assyria. The dinner also served to smooth out the Temple's fiscal year, bringing in regular donations at what had until then been a downtime. The brilliance of the idea had started his rise through the ranks, culminating in his selection as High Priest.

[The Commission cannot help but note that His Majesty's question indicates he did not know this piece of background, a disturbing ignorance of the inner workings of the priestly hierarchy. While we recognize that he has focused on creating more places of worship throughout the country, his failure to track priestly politics could be worrisome, leaving him less effective in dealing with this other branch of our national leadership.]

His Majesty continued. "What you probably do not know, however, is that Father and his advisers made a calculated decision to keep the extent of his illness secret. In fact, he was bedridden when the Assyrians were surrounding the city walls; he told me that he and his advisers feared that knowledge of that fact might have demoralized the nation enough to insist on surrendering."

[Note: The Commission, after long and contentious debate, has decided not to address the question of which health emergencies our monarchs and leaders must reveal to the public. Since this example is already moot, we can leave it for now. We do, however, urge empanelling a Commission to study the question.]

"When the Prophet came to visit, he informed Father the illness would be fatal. Pressed for a reason, he spoke of Father's refusal to marry and bear offspring. He knew, Isaiah said as he wagged a finger the way only a prophet can, of Hezekiah's fears about how his children would turn out, but that was not his place. Father's arrogating to himself the right to do so made his life forfeit.

"The rest of the story you seem to have uncovered. Mere minutes after leaving, the Prophet returned to say God had heard Father's tearful prayer, had decided to give him another fifteen years. And to show his faith in his prediction, Isaiah gave Father his daughter, and they married, producing an heir.

"Then they had their falling-out, when messengers came from Babylon congratulating Father on his military victory and on his healing. Of course, Father welcomed them and showed them around the Palace and Temple. Father spoke of the Prophet's rebuke afterward many times, both to warn Us not to run afoul of him, and because he was still incensed about it years later."

Menasseh allowed himself a self-deprecating smile. "All of which, We suppose, is a perhaps circuitous way of saying that if you have issues with Our grandfather that this Court needs to address, We are comfortable with our ability to be objective."

The news quickened Hilkiyah's mouth. "I understand and appreciate His Majesty's candor. I have struggled with whether to raise my concerns, with whether I will sound extreme, but my advisers have convinced me this is my sacred duty as guardian of this nation's religious spirit." He took a deep breath, readying himself for the plunge. "We at the Temple have come to believe that the time has come to try Isaiah for heresy, with capital punishment an option."

The king did not answer right away. He shifted in his throne, moved from lounging on an armrest to sitting straight up, thought another moment, then slumped back so that the curve of his back hit the wood of the throne. Then, the childhood slouch a posture the nation has not seen since his coronation, he straightened. After a few moments in that position, perhaps because of his rumored back issues, he stood to pace the room.

Finally, he turned to address the straight-backed man awaiting his response. "Much as We sympathize with your perspective, We hesitate. Our position requires Us to take account of the greater ramifications of such decisions. To begin only with the least important, the man has served this nation for decades, under trying circumstances. While We acknowledge the damage of his carping critiques, the Crown can never act rashly."

The High Priest nodded, trying with his excess vigor to convey how fully he understood. "Absolutely, we would need to proceed with care. The Temple can assure His Majesty that we will fully prove our claims against the Prophet before taking action. I merely wanted to check that the Palace was comfortable with our courts bringing him to justice for his religious failings."

The speed of the High Priest's words increased as he became more excited. Menasseh turned his head sideways and raised both hands, palms outward, slowing the conversation down, deliberating over each phrase. "Trying such a case at the Temple seems an error, as the only crimes likely to be proven fall outside your jurisdiction. It would seem that only Our Court has the leeway for what you suggest."

Now, he raised his voice, so the Court would hear and the scribe would know to enter it into the official minutes of the day. "We hereby grant Our Master High Priest and his staff the right to open an inquiry into the Prophet Isaiah. We note for the record that this extends to information gathering only, and comes with a warning to proceed with sensitivity, care, and speed. We expect to hear back with all sides of the story, including the views of all classes—especially the poor who so esteem him—and all peoples, Our nation's surrounding friends and allies."

The purse of Hilkiyah's lips was the only sign of dissatisfaction he allowed himself. "We cannot, Majesty, always take account of the mob. They flow to whoever gives them the most money at that moment. If Your Majesty were to time a tax reduction or an increase in funding for the bread kitchens to whatever action we might take against the Prophet, we would need not worry about their reaction."

Court watchers noted how Menasseh's two years on the throne had emboldened him; they swore he never would have questioned Hilkiyah's interests when his father first died. "Remind me, Master High Priest, why the Temple is so concerned with stamping out the Prophet's particular form of heresy?"

Hilkiyah snapped his fingers, and several attendants rushed forward with scrolls. Meeting His Majesty's eye, Hilkiyah raised his eyebrows and pointed his head at the table in front of the monarch, a mute request to approach and be heard. When the king assented, the High Priest unfolded the papyri and launched into the lecture he gives each incoming class of student-priests. Even so, witnesses went out of their way to comment on his passion, how much it sounded as if it was his first time.

"The Torah made the mistake of thinking the Temple could be fully supported by the yearly poll tax. Long experience and careful record keeping—see, here and here, those figures go all the way back to Aviyam, son of Rehavam—have taught us that sacrifices are the backbone of our Temple economy. Without the accompanying gifts, it would be difficult and perhaps impossible to effectively intervene with our Father in Heaven on behalf of our brethren. Only when our stomachs are sated, we find, can we teach God's laws and ways to others."

Those closest to the king caught his glance at Hilkiyah's belly, his uplifted eyebrow telling those who knew him that he was wondering how much meat it took to fill a container of that size.

"That explains our concern over the Prophet. In brief, Majesty, our figures show the damage Isaiah has caused us, how much harder he has made it to inspire the people's fealty to the proper service of God. We have three graphs: the first correlates the number of sacrifices and the number of priests on duty. We ascribe that to the personal factor, people's greater interest in bringing offerings when they know a friend or relative will perform the ritual. We always tell trainees that simply mentioning to friends, family, and even acquaintances the date of one's next service almost invariably helps with quota, since a few people will decide to give when they hear that news.

"The second graph shows the relationship between offering sacrifices and greater religiosity in general; as you can see, those who offer more are also more likely to attend worship more often, and to support the priests more generously as well.

"The third graph, the troubling one, tracks the connection between hearing Isaiah speak and offering a sacrifice in the next thirty days. We followed three populations, those who had not heard Isaiah, those who heard him once or twice, and those who hear him regularly. As you can see from the red line, his regulars are five or ten sacrifices *a month* behind the other groups, on average."

Menasseh waited to be sure the presentation was over. When the silence lengthened, he said, "These figures alarm Us indeed, and the Crown expresses its gratitude to the Temple for bringing this matter to Our attention. However, the fullness of time has led Us to alter Our earlier judgment. Given the Temple's stake in this matter, it would seem clear the Crown must conduct the investigation as well as the trial."

Hilkiyah's face betrayed no reaction to losing control over the issue. His only voiced concern was, "Can His Majesty give any sense of when the Palace's inquiry would conclude? We at the Temple would hate to see it linger."

Menasseh waved off the question, purring, "We understand your anxiety, and assure you that We will give this matter our most expeditious attention. Let us try for a trial in two months—We trust you would make yourself available to repeat these and any other relevant facts?"

With a nod and a bow, the High Priest assented and left.

The meeting alone justifies many of our conclusions, and those interested can flip to that section of this report. However, in deference to a vocal minority of Commission members, we also include information we have gathered about two debriefings that took place following this meeting.

Hilkiyah started his review as soon as he got back to the Temple grounds. Several advisers glowed as they testified about these sessions, praising his generosity at mentoring others by taking them through each of his actions, explaining why and how he decided to act as he did.

Although these were some of the same people passed over when he was elected, his consistent assistance in furthering their careers has won them over, as far as this Commission could tell. More than one quoted his oft-repeated reminder that he would not live forever, that opportunities are almost always unexpected, and his urging each of them to always be ready in case the Divine Will, and the vote of the other priests, selects him as the next Temple leader.

The open environment encouraged questions, such as, "What did you mean by blood relationship between the king and the Prophet?"

All heads turned, some shocked at the man's temerity, but most at his ignorance. The wedding had taken place only eighteen years earlier, making it hard to believe even a thirty-year-old priest would have forgotten. Hilkiyah ignored the interruption, certain someone else would whisper the answer to the embarrassed priest.

The next question was more challenging. The priest who always sits three seats to the High Priest's right began haltingly—[please note: the Temple invoked its executive privilege, asking that we keep identifying marks out of this report, so attendees at such meetings could feel comfortable saying whatever they wanted, without worry that it would later be tied to them in public]—trying to balance his desire for knowledge with his fear of speaking out of turn.

"Granted that Master High Priest wished to approach His Majesty about the Prophet, I wonder how My Master could know His Majesty would react positively. Especially considering their family ties..." He trailed off, hoping he had been clear enough, without needing to get more explicit.

Hilkiyah smiled. "I did the same as you; you may not have noticed, but I did not end my first question to

143

His Majesty. I mentioned the relationship, and let the question hang, to see the reaction. It's a very important point, though, so I thank you for giving me the chance to stress it. It is vital, always, to gauge the person with whom you are speaking. If you try to push an idea they dislike or reject, you'll never get anywhere."

This prompted another hand farther down the table. "Would that be why the High Priest has not reproached the king about the altars he is building throughout the Land? Would we not want to urge him to stop harming the Temple's centrality?"

At this question, the table split between looks of scorn from those who understood the High Priest's strategy and nods of agreement from those who had been wondering the same.

Hilkiyah fingered his beard, pondering how to respond. "I see our Prophet has made inroads here as well. It would be convenient to believe that all sacrifices have to come to the Temple, convenient as well as lucrative. But we have to remember that God fills the whole world with His Presence. We would be wrong to limit His worship to one place."

He shook his head as if to clear it. "But that's not the whole point, either. Some around this table are apparently falling behind in reading the latest studies, which confirm our tradition and experience. Once people are drawn to religion, no matter what kind or what god is being worshiped, they will come to the Temple as well. I do not remonstrate with His Majesty because his altar building, whether for God or Baal, cannot but be good for the Temple. How is it the advertisements say it?"

The Temple memorizer chimed in. "A god in every house, a sacrifice from every family."

Hilkiyah nodded. "Correct. Rising religious activity floats all boats, ours along with the others."

Custom dictated that Hilkiyah go around the table, starting with the priest farthest from him. "Yes?"

"I don't know if my question is proper, and I do not wish to speak out of turn—"

Hilkiyah cut in with a smile. "If you do not ask, you cannot learn. Open your mouth, my son, and let us all be edified."

The younger man nodded, gulped, and then rushed his words out, as if he feared he might lose his courage if he waited. "Well, I was curious as to why My Master let His Majesty ramble on about what happened so long ago with Hezekiah and Isaiah. Once we knew His Majesty had no deep feelings for the Prophet, why not get right to the trial?'

Hilkiyah nodded in approval. "A good issue to raise. You see," he paused, finger reproving the now blushing priest, smile taking the edge off the reproach, "had you indulged your bashful side, you would have stolen this insight from yourself and your brothers around this table. I was tempted to do as you say, but I reminded myself of a simple rule. Can anyone guess what it was?"

Voices came from all around the table. "Never interrupt royalty." "The King's anger is always just under the surface." "What's a few minutes in the name of harmony?"

The High Priest's head bobbed to encourage each suggestion, but none earned the point of a finger and raise of eyebrows that meant the person had hit on the answer he had intended. "All good points, but here's another one: information is always valuable. His Majesty told me of matters I had never known. I cannot say when I will use that knowledge, only that I will. If my experience counts for anything," he looked around the table to be sure they caught the humor, "any fact learned will one day be put to use."

He glanced out the window, gauging the direction of the shadows. "I can take one more question, then must bring this pleasant interlude to a close. It is almost time for my afternoon flour offering."

The reminder of the meeting's approaching end lifted the hands of those who had not yet spoken, hoping to get their names or faces into the High Priest's consciousness. Opportunities for advancement arose suddenly; speaking up was one of the few proven methods of keeping oneself in line for whatever might come.

Hilkiyah pointed to the priest who waved least obtrusively. Surprised his half-raised hand had gotten noticed, he looked around before speaking, wanting to be sure it was indeed he who had been chosen. "At earlier meetings, I had the impression we were focused on managing the trial ourselves. Was there a reason it was conceded to the Palace?"

The High Priest grimaced and looked off into space as he thought about his answer. "An excellent question; that was the one outcome I found less than fully pleasing. The king's resistance surprised me, is the truth. He never would have done that when he first came onto the throne."

Without quite finishing his answer, he rose, walking around the table, shaking hands or tapping people on the shoulder as he made his way to the door. The men around the table perked up, trying to offer a memorable good-bye. Hilkiyah reached the door and delivered his exit line. "Given his feelings, the value of keeping His Majesty's goodwill outweighed my interest in hosting the trial. That concession, I assure you, will mean the trial goes as we want it. His Majesty will ensure it."

The door closed behind him, leaving a circle of admirers again awed by the savvy their leader brought to the complexities of his position.

The postmeeting analysis at the Palace had none of that collegiality. After the priestly retinue left, the king adjourned to the small conference area on the other side of a small door in the Throne Room. Twelve advisers were already assembled around the wooden table that had been there since King Solomon's time. Testimony before this Commission told of the terror inspired by sitting in a seat engraved with the names of all the giants who had previously occupied it, let alone the kingly stare that met them this day.

"Remind Us, please, who prepared the briefing for today's meeting, the one that bore no hint the priests would suggest a trial?"

The ice in his voice hit them all, instinct causing a few to rub their upper arms for warmth. The second in command spoke up. "I briefed His Majesty, as always."

The king was not to be diverted. He turned to the Minister, his emphasis carrying the rebuke. "Which was why We were careful to ask who *prepared* it."

A hand went up, only partially raised. "I did, Majesty."

The speaker, largely unknown to the public, is a legend in Palace circles. He had passed his sixtieth year, including thirty-five sitting at that table, with three different monarchs. Those three words, however, brought his unparalleled streak to an end.

The king turned his stare on him. "Was there a reason We were not readied for the suggestion that Our grandfather be put on trial?"

The man hung his head, as did those around him, afraid of being asked for their opinions. Speaking to the

147

floor, he said, "We had no advance warning, Majesty. The High Priest has managed to purge or win over any of those who heretofore gave us advance information. My sources have all told me they could no longer imagine betraying his confidence. I apologize for the momentary discomfort this caused…"

The grin on the royal face, limited to lips and teeth, washed over the group, setting off their internal alarms; sensing the change, the man speaking glanced up, saw his monarch's face, looked back down, and tried another tack. The others, already cowering, shivered themselves down lower in their seats. Before he could speak, the king did.

"We recognize this was an honest mistake and are willing to give another chance of service to the Crown."

The hint that he might escape punishment brought his eyes up, hope dawning. "Yes, Majesty, that would be wonderful!"

A satisfied nod from the king. "Your dedication is much appreciated. As it happens, an occasion to put it to the test has presented itself. We have this morning received a request for an ambassador to the Babylonian port town of Nehardea, she of the freezing winters and oppressive summers. It is Our inclination to make this ambassadorship permanent and hereditary. Serve well, and We might be convinced to revisit the question in, say, twenty years, hmmm?"

Several of those at the table testified that their own faces burned red on hearing the sentence. The man himself blanched as the words worked their ways from his ears to his brain, as he contemplated telling his family they were moving to a hole-in-the-wall somewhere in Babylonia. He opened his mouth, thinking to beg for mercy, but shut it when he saw the king's face, when he saw how his now former friends refused to meet his gaze.

Instead, he bent at the waist, eyes fixed on the floor, said, "Thank you, Majesty, for this opportunity," and left, bowed body pointed toward his monarch at all times.

Menasseh waited until he was gone, then turned to the others. "Father wasted most of our time together trying to convince me of his narrow and provincial view of how to worship God." The shift to personal reminiscence was so rare that it pushed aside all thoughts of the departed council member. The king made eye contact with each adviser, the pause stressing that his choice of words was conscious and intentional.

"Occasionally, though, he imparted a few useful tips on how to rule. One of the best was the reminder that whenever you see someone act out of character, the first objective must be to understand that person's motives."

He paused, waiting for the light to dawn. Soon enough, one of the men around the table nodded. "Yes, you understand?"

"I suppose it sounded to me like His Majesty found the High Priest's behavior surprising, leading him to wonder about his unstated agenda."

The pleasure on their ruler's face encouraged the rest. A younger man, three seats over, raised his hand to add, "Right, why go after Isaiah *now*? How much could one man be affecting the sacrificial service anyway?"

The Minister of Internal Security objected. "Actually, quite a bit. Remember that he is of the royal family. His powers of persuasion are inborn, and his training only intensified them. Day to day you might not notice it, but our figures agree with the Temple's; over the past decades, the Prophet has made recognizable inroads into the priests' wealth. There's no need to cry for them, but remember that forty years ago, they could expect fresh vestments each day in the Temple and sacrificial meat for dinner, if not lunch too. Besides those cutbacks, the Temple has also had to limit the number of priests allowed to serve out of rotation. For those used to the earlier amenities, this reduction cannot be pleasant."

He paused, weighing the wisdom of bringing up information that distracted from the Palace's stated goals. "On the other hand, the High Priest neglected to mention, perhaps did not know of, more positive aspects of his legacy. We in Internal Security see Isaiah as the source of a reduction in violent crime—the more he speaks, the fewer deadbeats' limbs get broken by loan sharks. The connection is even stronger for homicides traced back to defaulted debts."

His Majesty waved off the digression. "Granted he is not all evil, We are discussing the Temple's interest in the matter. Were it only about sacrifices, We would have expected them to complain about the altar-rebuilding program as well. Their cooperation with Our attempts on that front leaves Us to wonder why the Prophet bothers them so?"

The lack of agenda was rattling the attendees. Witnesses told this Commission of their surprise that His Majesty was giving the encounter with the High Priest more than its usual perfunctory review. Brainstorming with His Majesty was a gamble, with the possibility of impressing the king, but without any immunity for saying something stupid. By this point, chairs were shifting and scraping around the room as the discomfort worked its way out as nervous motion.

Finally, one suggested, "It *was* interesting to see how long Hilkiyah stayed in the Palace. He has on other occasions spoken of how he counts the moments away from the Temple, of his fear of some accidental impurity forcing him to stay out of the Temple for the remainder of the day."

Someone snorted. "Your point?"

The first speaker glared. "My *point* was that His Majesty must be correct; the High Priest had more at stake here than just the Prophet himself."

Silence followed as the table pondered the mystery. After several minutes, the youngest, only twenty-two, risked a suggestion. He told the Commission he had only tried because he knew he would be replaced as soon as an older candidate became available anyway. Courage, he told us, comes from having nothing to lose.

"Perhaps he's tired of Isaiah's claiming he knows the right way to serve God. Hilkiyah might not mind His Majesty's initiatives because they are so pluralistic. But Isaiah? He directly opposes what they say God wants; it must drive them crazy."

Several others jumped in to support him, parental instincts calling them to protect the vulnerable young. The loudest said, "Just the other day, Majesty, I saw a priest teaching the laws of tithing. He was fascinating, showing how some tithes are taken by estimation while others must be calculated with a measuring tool.

"I could see how well he was doing, how his listeners were absorbing the information to implement it in the future. Until someone sitting there said he had just heard Isaiah talking about the priests' misuse of funds, and what did he have to say about that? I thought a vein would pop in the poor man's head."

"Majesty?" It was the Royal Guardian, the man who had guided His Majesty's education and training from youth.

The king's body language changed from imperial to deferential. "Yes?" The word "master" started to come out, but he caught himself.

"Perhaps we might reconsider the trial. After all, if we are so suspicious of the motives underlying the suggestion, we might decide to let it slide. He's not a young man, this prophet, and how many last longer than forty years, anyway?"

The king was already moving his head back and forth. "No, no, out of the question. Regardless of what pushed him to bring it up, the High Priest made points We are duty-bound to pursue. We will simply have to keep Our focus on two fronts, on this trial and then on keeping the Temple staff in check."

The king looked around at his inner circle again, the stern monarch replaced by the skilled leader who could let each one feel the full weight of his liege's confidence that he could achieve the great tasks expected of him.

His silent message delivered, His Majesty closed with a verbalized note of caution. "Remember to tie up all loose ends. Hilkiyah might not care about the general populace, but it is Our sacred duty to do so. Remember that they see the Prophet as some kind of hero." He shook his head and rolled his eyes. "As if he ever tried to collect loans or had to contemplate the economic consequences of widespread defaults! Just be sure there are no glitches or missteps; this case must come before Us in airtight form. Are We clear?"

All heads nodded as the king added, a smile playing at his lips, edging into his voice, "Or do Our Babylonian friends need more ambassadors?"

III. The Trial: Exhaustive interviews have convinced the Commission that little in the next six months was worth recording or analyzing in any detail. The occasional examples of excessive zeal in readying witnesses for trial have been referred to the Office of Internal Security, but have no place in a public document.

The investigation largely confirmed the High Priest's predictions. Painstaking fact-checking yielded little more than the charges originally filed: the Prophet insistently worked to reduce people's interest in sacrifice, to convince them that his was the only right way to worship. The Temple accountant's sworn testimony on the decrease in the surplus was almost superfluous.

The only meaningful additions to the prosecution's case were the missives solicited from the foreign ministers of our allies and enemies, Ishmaelites to the south, Moab, Kedar, and, farthest away, Bavel. This awe-inspiring outpouring, unanimous in its antipathy to the Prophet, can be found in the Palace archives. We reproduce one example to give a sense of how the letters went:

> To Menasseh, son of Hezekiah, scion of David, Greetings and Peace!
>
> We welcome your initiative in soliciting our view of Isaiah, son of Amotz, whom your father insisted on calling Prophet. Indeed, we urge you to do so more often; consistent adherence to such a policy cannot but produce more cohesive relations, and help us avoid future unpleasantness.
>
> As to the matter itself: Your prophet has been a thorn in our side since the time of your paternal grandfather. He has meddled in our relations with each of your predecessors, advising them to take rash and foolish actions. Only by the wildest of coincidences have your people avoided the consequences of his ill-informed and ill-conceived foreign policy. Caution in your relations with stronger nations would be advised,

especially when our gods are so much stronger than yours.

We note with pleasure your willingness to free yourself of this insidious influence, and look forward to hearing that you have opened a door to an era of friendly cooperation between our nations!

Signed,
Rav Shakeh, writing for His Majesty, the Mighty Hand of the gods, Sargon

The Commission notes the impact of these letters in the trial. As Selomiel, Undersecretary of the Foreign Office, said when he presented them at trial, "May it please the Court, the Foreign Ministry notes, first of all, how much ill will our prophet has engendered. *He* may not care that we have to live with these people, do business with them, avoid war with them, but the rest of us cannot dismiss the issue so lightly.

"Second, we urge the Court to recognize that such unanimity cannot but indicate truth. When have *all* the nations of the world agreed on a matter without its being right?"

The defense's vigorous counterattack deserves mention, if only because we admire courage in the face of certain failure. As heads around the room nodded at the prosecution's summation, the defense attorney rose. Before speaking, he bent to listen to his master. The Prophet whispered energetically, his disciple gave a short jerk of the head, and then regaled the Court with a sermon in Isaiah's mold, arguing that our nation walks its own path, does not adhere to the values or rules of others.

Well articulated as it was, it had already then been dulled by overuse. Numerous witnesses told of wondering when the Prophet and his group would accept that theory was all well and good, but that even we Israelites also had to admit when the rest of the world was right.

The defense's second argument was an even less fortunate choice of strategy. In a climate where we are all beginning to realize just how broad the worship of supreme beings can be, a more astute legal team would have convinced the defendant not to bother relying on his claim that his prophecies were the single acceptable version of truth.

Their further arguments were at least more interesting, as they attempted to show that the prosecution's evidence proved less than claimed. To rebut the prosecution's graphs, the defense gave a lesson in statistics. An excerpt of the trial's testimony will show how successfully defense counsel separated correlation from causation.

Defense: You testified Isaiah has led to a reduction in sacrifices?

Temple Expert: Not quite. My testimony was that sacrifices drop when he is around and speaking in public.

D: But you want the Court to draw conclusions from that.

T: Well, yes, sure. Think of it this way: if he goes someplace, speaks out against sacrifice, and then donations to the Temple drop—well, you do the math.

D: Are you aware that Elijah the Prophet told the Northern Kingdom there would be no rain as long as they worshiped idols? And the rain ceased for the next three years?

T: Yes.

D: Would you say that proved he was right?

T: No, obviously not.

D: Because?

T: Well, for one thing, because the rain came back.

D: At what point?

T: What do you mean?

D: I mean, what did Elijah do *before* the rain came back?

T: Announced its return. But still…

D: Thank you. Let us move to a different example. Do you recall the sun moving back over the Temple steps some years ago?

T: Yes, during King Hezekiah's time.

D: Do you recall how the king himself understood the event?

T: He thought it showed he would live for fifteen more years.

D: Can you tell the Court why he thought that?

T: Isaiah had told him that's what it meant.

D: And how many years did he live?

T: Fifteen.

D: Would you say the correlation proved Isaiah is a prophet of God to whom we must always listen?

T: No, not at all. He may have been correct on that and other occasions, but that does not mean…

And so it went; much as most observers understood the truth of the Temple expert's points, they squirmed with him under the defense counsel's skilled lawyering. Also helpful were the economic factors the defense cited. Using Palace economists to describe the current economic malaise was brilliant, leaving it to the Court to realize that when people are poorer, they might offer fewer sacrifices even without the input of a prophet.

Sociologists came next, with their theory that the recovery from the Assyrian invasion had inspired a new economic conservatism, a focus on savings to the detriment of incidental expenses such as sacrifices. Their detailed statistics on the rise in the savings rate was, to many observers, a moment when the defense seemed in danger of winning. If people were hoarding every penny for fear of a new attack, everyone in the courtroom knew Isaiah could not be solely blamed for the drop in donations.

In desperation, the prosecuting attorney secured Court permission to introduce rebuttal evidence. The key to his success was convincing the Court to allow him to pretend he was standing for the defense. Each of the impoverished witnesses, thinking they were helping their prophet, delighted in answering his questions. They glowed as they told of how much their lives had been eased by giving up peace offerings, how it had freed them to pay down their loans, interest, and principle.

[We cannot but pause to note the tragedy of innocent people misled by a man who bears the mantle of prophecy. His encouraging their materialism, using their money for personal needs rather than to serve the Creator, is astonishing. Much as we have avoided editorializing, we cannot help but say, Woe to the ears that have heard this!]

The defense might yet have regrouped but for the coup de grace, the affidavit the prosecution filed from Serayah, city editor for *Temple News and Report.* Available from the Commission as a separate document, the affidavit in sum tells of Serayah's increasing frustrations at training new reporters to resist the lure of Isaiah's ideas. His closing, that he had retired from his job and was heading south to his family plot, highlighted how hard he had found working in a city in which the Prophet held sway.

This Commission heard multiple witnesses' testimony on the affidavit's effect. The argument about the Prophet's impact on the Temple was one type of issue; to hear that he was the reason valuable citizens could no longer stand to serve society raised the specter of a whole different type of threat. That was the moment all in the Court saw the inevitable, that the danger had to be excised from our midst.

IV. Passing of Sentence and Execution: His Majesty bowed his head for long moments after the reading of the affidavit, raising them only to look at his grandfather. Defense counsel opened his mouth, stopped by a royal glance and a prophet's staying hand. Menasseh's voice, when he spoke, boomed with the full authority of his office. "Isaiah, Prophet of Israel, have you anything more to say in your defense?"

Until that point, witnesses agreed, the Prophet had been a model of careful grooming, tunic freshly pressed, white beard cut to look full yet impeccably neat. The eyes with which he scanned the courtroom burned with the same fire as on the city's streets. And the head, cocked to the side, communicated a mind deep in thought, presumably on how he could avoid the fate to which he was being drawn.

As the king addressed him, the Prophet's robust body seemed to have shrunk, the tunic suddenly loose enough to fall into disarray. His eyes, their fire doused by tears, glistened in a way that suggested to some that he had already placed a foot into the World to Come.

He took his time, then said only, "Don't do this, Menasseh." The king's stony countenance moved him to add, "Those who seek God, grandson, will find ever-greater strength. But those who set themselves against God..."

Menasseh's smile had more than a little pain in it. "Against God? Grandfather," there was, by all accounts, an audible intake of breath at the king's piercing the wall between official position and blood relations, "you wander our city preaching in opposition to what our Master Moses said, and you speak of those who set themselves against God?"

The challenge brought the Prophet back to himself. Eyes flashing, his voice strengthened as he said, "I? Speak against our Teacher Moses? Take away your fixation with sacrifices, and where have I diverged from the Torah?"

The Education Minister has told this Commission that the rest of the confrontation will become a mandatory part of the curriculum in schools throughout the country. It is not every day or decade that a king matches a prophet word for word in Scripture. The most diehard of the Prophet's defenders looked away when faced with the contrasts between Isaiah's claims to have seen God and the Torah's unequivocal declaration that no one can see Him and live. Almost as bad was his implying that God hears our cries only at certain times, clearly contradicted by Moses' promise that God answers whenever we call.

By this point, Court observers began filing out. The tension that had drawn them was gone, replaced by the pathos of a grandson forced to save the nation from a stubborn religious deviant who happened to be his grandfather. Few could bear to watch; we as a Commission cannot stomach the details of the rest. Suffice it to say that Isaiah, son of Amotz, was buried that day in his family plot.

V. Conclusions: Assembling the facts of this episode cannot but sadden anyone involved, and we are no exception. Before we register our conclusions, we remind readers of our own human frailties, the limitations of our abilities to reconstruct what occurred, and the likelihood that we have missed some aspects that might have nuanced our conclusions. None should think we present our views as the final word, but a judge has only what his eyes can see.

Even having been granted the freedom to do so, we find nothing to critique in His Majesty's conduct. We are stunned by our king's courage in facing the truth about his grandfather; we can only pray our nation will always be blessed with rulers so invested in the right and good. Similarly, we are impressed with his accepting the High Priest's lead in embarking on this investigation. A king who remains so open to input from others gives us hope that his reign will be long and fruitful for us all.

Finally, it was His Majesty's familiarity with the Prophet's published works that saved us from the division an inconclusive trial would have produced. Without his taking the time to find where his grandfather had stepped outside tradition, our people might have suffered a continuing controversy over the justice administered here. Happy are the people with Menasseh as ruler!

In turning to the High Priest, we stay first with the positive. His going to the Palace for approval, fostering cooperation between Temple and Palace, contributed to minimizing the wound this incident caused our people. This lack of territoriality will be crucial to building even greater bonds in the weeks and months to come.

That having been said, this Commission must note some distressing overtones of residual turf-mindedness.

We wonder, for example, why the priests themselves had not noticed how Isaiah had contradicted the Torah. We are left to worry that the Prophet was at least right in terms of the Temple functionaries, that they have let themselves focus too narrowly on sacrifices in the religious leadership they provide.

The High Priest's astute political instincts also worry us; savoir faire, necessary for attaining and retaining position, may sometimes shade over into sticking only to his own goals and ambitions. We urge Our Master Hilkiyah to be on the alert for that trap.

If we might make a recommendation to His Majesty, we would wonder whether family history can sometimes limit our horizons by defining our direction, leaving us too prone to following or rebelling against that legacy. We hope His Majesty will not only rectify his father's failings, as with his inspiringly eclectic interest in the wealth of deities, but that he will also address the range of problems facing our nation.

As for the deceased Prophet, we can only hang our heads in sorrow. That a man with such early promise should go so far astray is a cautionary tale. We recommend continued days of fasting and repentance to remind ourselves of the fine line that worshiping the gods requires us to walk.

We append to this report the obituary from *Temple News and Report*, written by Me-ka-el, whose byline reads Mike, son of Jack; given what his editor, Seraya, said about his early devotion to Isaiah, his more mature perspective allows some hope that the Prophet's damage will yet be undone, that we can yet produce a society more punctilious about fulfillment of the laws of the sacrifices, and more fully serving the gods.

Isaiah Dies; King's Cousin Mourned and Scorned

Chances are, as you read this obituary, you have intense emotions. His emotional impact on all who heard him may be the most memorable aspect of Isaiah's long career.

A cousin of the royal family, the young Isaiah could have settled into a life of wealth and privilege, attending feasts at the private altars of the members of his social circle. His choice of the solitary life set him apart early on. As his elementary school teacher remarked yesterday when this reporter contacted him, "Already back then, you could see that he would tread his own path, regardless of consequences."

His independent spirit earned him accolades but also freed him to arrive at mistaken ideas about how to worship God, culminating in his own grandson overseeing his execution.

The lower classes of society, particularly widows and orphans, crowded the streets for his funeral procession, crying and calling out, "Master Isaiah, who will speak for us now?"

More responsible sources noted the difficulty of evaluating his legacy. The official Palace statement read:

"His Majesty recognizes his debt to the departed, without whom King Hezekiah would never have married. His Majesty is profoundly saddened that the Prophet's many transgressions forced his hand.

"In recognition of the tragedy of this event, His Majesty declares the morrow of the next Sabbath a national day of mourning. All males over the age of twenty must go to their town square, where the priests will lead a program of sacrifice, prayer, and fasting. To honor the Prophet's memory, no loans may be collected that day."

The Temple chose its words with equal care. The spokesman said only: "In the words the Prophet immortalized thirty years ago, we respond to his passing by praying that 'Death will be swallowed forever, and the Lord God will wipe away all tears from all faces.' May the Lord judge us all, including Isaiah, for peace."

Perhaps most sadly, the troubles of the Prophet's later years may have wiped away the memory of his early successes, the close cooperation between him and the late king through the first half of that reign. Rumor has it that the ardor later waned because the Prophet insisted on meddling in foreign policy. Others ground his fall from grace in the embarrassing revelations of his failure to participate in sacrificial rites.

Whatever the cause, many have noted the loneliness of his life. In addition to long periods of voluntary isolation, his prophecies aroused more anger than followers. His few devotees knew that to be an "Isaiah-man" meant stepping outside of sophisticated society. Few were willing to admit that they accepted his simplistic view of a world run by one God, Who prefers good deeds to sacrifice.

With his death, the tear he rent in our national fabric can heal, as we reunite around our king and the worships he promotes. Nonetheless, all who read this obituary may want to bow their heads in respect for Isaiah's efforts, misguided as they may have been.

Isaiah b. Amotz, Prophet, executed for treason and heresy yesterday, after a forty-year career.

5/9, THE AFTERMATH

The boy leaped into bed, landing facedown, head pointed toward the wall, right leg lifted to his side at ninety degrees, the position in which he would later fall asleep. Then, having reminded himself he knew how to do it, he flipped over onto his back, arms and legs at his sides, and waited with a smile.

His father reached for the blanket folded at the end of the bed, stretched it out to its full length, and placed it under the boy's chin, smoothing it all the way back. He was especially careful it made its way over each of the boy's toes, a ritual he would need to repeat after story time. The nights he didn't do it right, the boy called him back, usually at the exact moment he had managed to get himself settled into his evening work.

Placing the half-empty jug of milk by the boy's head, he leaned over and recited the bedtime prayer, hoping that by the time of his next birthday, his eleventh, the boy would agree to say it himself. At least he recited the last verse with him. The father reminded the son to drink the milk before it went sour, and kissed him. He stood and moved to leave, but a giggle from the bed stopped him.

Turning back, eyebrows raised, he said, "Yes?"

A chuckle now, louder, less stifled. "You forgot to tell me the story!"

The father looked puzzled. "Story?"

The boy was laughing full out. "Daaaaad, stop with the jokes! The story!"

The father sighed heavily, made a show of dragging himself back to sit on the side of the camel hide suspended between four posts. Smoothing out the blanket near him, he asked, "What story do you want to hear?"

The boy squealed with joy at the successful completion of the pre-story routine. As he kicked and shook his whole body, he said, "You know!"

The father settled in, lying down next to his son, their heads touching as they did each night. "All right, all right. Where were we? Oh, yes, I've got it."

Jer woke up, the morning words of thanks springing to his lips, fifty years of reciting them having brought him full circle from needing to think before each one to running through them without any thought and, finally, back to experiencing real gratitude for God having given him another day. Checking his mouth for any taste of prophecy, he shook his head, turned to the wall, and scratched an eighth mark, one for each day of futility since the delegation had come to him.

Knowing they might make their morning visit before he had a chance to compose himself, he quickly washed his hands and prayed, thoughts too jumbled for any moments of Presence to soothe his battered psyche. It was as he was taking three steps back, body always facing the Ruins, that the knock confirmed his sense of timing.

Opening the door, he saw the same group of forty or forty-five who had eight days ago begged for his input. Standing at the front were the Kereach boys, John slightly in front, his confidence unaffected by having failed to protect their leader from the assassin's sword. Jer turned to the others and said, "I know how anxious you all are; I am too. But I have not yet had Word, I'm sorry."

Protocol gave them little option but to bow their heads, say, "We thank you for your time, Master," and turn away. Jer closed his door, and the group moved two hundred paces away, to review the interaction.

Az spoke first. "It's like I've been saying; he's washed up, done with, over. It's not coming; we just have to make a decision ourselves."

His brother, Jazz, disagreed. "You know, we didn't set a time limit or anything. I don't even know if you *can* set a time limit. If it hasn't come yet, it hasn't come, but I don't see how that changes the commitment we made."

John said, "Commitment?"

Jonathan, the other Kereach son, said, "Sure, commitment. We went and asked him what God thought about going to Egypt or staying, and we *said*—here's the commitment part—that we'd obey whatever we were told. So I'm with Jazz; we wait until we hear."

Az shook his head. "It was a mistake, I told you that from the beginning. All he knows how to do is tell us how bad we are and what's going to go wrong. We should never have told him he could have that kind of power over our future. He'll use it, string us along until he thinks he's losing us, and then recommend a plan that puts him in the driver's seat. That's what he's wanted this whole time anyway."

John liked a divided group; it gave him a clear and accomplishable leadership role. "All right, so we have some here who seem to think we were mistaken in trusting Jer, that we should make this decision on our own. Is that right?"

Twenty heads nodded. "And some who think that nothing important has changed, that eight days ago, we told him we need the Word and would trust whatever he told us, and we just have to wait. Is *that* right?"

Fifteen heads bobbed up and down. John noted the percentages, filing the information away. "Meanwhile, there's a great deal of work to be done either way. Let's get back to our jobs; we have until at least tomorrow for his answer, if there is one."

Some grumbles began, the crowd unhappy about leaving the dilemma for yet another wearing day. John held up a hand to quiet them, continuing as if he had been pausing, not finishing. "At the same time, the Executive Committee will pay a visit to Priest Pasher. We'll see what he has to say about our friend Jer, and that may help us decide what to do if tomorrow is no better than today. Agreed?"

Seeing the easing of the tension on the faces in front of him, he got down to details. "All right, then. In the name of fairness, I'm revising the work groupings. I want you, you, and," his finger hovered as he thought of who would best fit that group, "you, on the Mount, overseeing the clearing of the rubble. If we're going to stay, there's no way we can allow the Ruins to simply sit there, accusing us. People are already complaining, wanting to know how long we will let the Destruction of the Temple stare us in the face.

"And then the four of you," they were standing together, so he identified them with one sweep of his hand, "take over the group making the preparations for the move. The rest please go to the countryside, take stock of the farms. I want a good sense of what we're up against if we decide to stay."

They headed out, and the Executive Committee went to the priest. In the poorer part of town, where Jer lived, there was little for the Disaster to have made worse, but the signs of what had happened became harder to avoid as the group passed the shells of the once beautiful houses that dotted Pasher's street. At his home, the solid wood door had been smashed in several spots, so John could simply call through instead of knocking.

A voice from inside answered, "Coming, coming, coming!"

He opened the door, his red-rimmed eyes less of a shock than the scratches on his arms. To see a priest unconcerned with covering the evidence of his having torn at his skin in his mourning was more than they had expected. Three Committee members broke down, leaving it to Az to answer the priest's querying look.

"Master Priest, we wondered whether we might have a word with you about Jer."

His eyebrows furrowed. "Jer, as in Jeremiah?"

Their heads nodded in response. "Well, I suppose, but I can't see what you think I have to say about that. Well, anyway, come in, come in."

They filed in, each stifling his gasps. They had been here before 5/9, even in the worst days of the siege, but the house had never looked like this. Pasher seemed to have made no efforts to rebuild, or even to sweep away the devastation wrought by the rampaging soldiers.

Less surprising, there were no longer chairs or even animal hides to cover the floor. Taking seats in the dirt, they waited for Pasher to join them at the head of the circle they had formed. Once he had, Az spoke again.

"I'm not sure how much you know or want to about what's going on, but the short story is that we need your expert opinion about Jeremiah."

The Pasher who had answered the door had looked much like any other Jerusalemite these days, weary and wary, every movement weighed with grief and tentative, as if about to touch a stove of unknown temperature. As Az's message sank in, being asked for advice brought out vestiges of his professional demeanor.

171

His voice dropped, and he again exuded the seriousness of mind and purpose expected of a counselor. He asked, "And what makes you think I have anything to offer in that area?"

John had recovered enough to reassert himself. "Come on, you know and we know that he consulted with you for years. We've got to imagine it gave you some insight into the man."

Pasher gave several little half nods, letting them know how judicious he was in considering this information. "Granting, for the sake of the argument, that that is true, you must know that anything said to me in those conversations is privileged, and that I could never reveal them to you."

Eli, the youngest of the group, had had enough, and burst out, "Privileged! What kind of idiot are you? Do you not see the Ruins? You think professional confidentiality matters anymore, let alone being more important than figuring out our next step?"

John's smile could have been his way of signaling his benign tolerance of the rashness of youth, or his pleasure that someone else had said what he could never have allowed himself to. Either way, he spoke now to smooth over Pasher's ruffled feathers.

"What my younger colleague means is that your information could be vital to our national future. It might also help your conscience if I tell you that we would not be looking for specifics of conversations you and Jer had, so you wouldn't have to violate that therapeutic promise. We're just looking for general impressions as to his status."

Pasher said, "Status?"

Eli had composed himself, so John gave him a nod to invite him to pick up the thread. "Sure. Is he now, still, an active prophet, or has the Power left him? Is it common for him to seek a prophecy and have to wait more than eight days for a reply? Should we assume that the prophecies he reports are always accurate? If not, what is his mental health; can we trust that his visions are always the Word, or might he have other kinds of episodes that also produce prophecies? And finally, most importantly for some of us, is he under the sway of those who might influence him wrongly?"

Pasher raised his eyebrows. "Such as?"

The father paused, noticing his son's eyes fluttering, sleep overtaking him. As soon as his father's voice ceased, though, the boy popped awake, and said, "Don't stop!"

The father sighed. "All right, but that's pretty much the end of that conversation. They told Pasher who they thought might be telling Master Jer what to do, and Pasher said he'd review his notes and give them his answer the next day."

The boy was more animated now, the opposite of what his father had sought. "Wait, wait, wait, I don't get it. *Who* did they think might be getting Master Jer to lie about his prophecies?"

The father sighed. "Well, if you ask, me."

The boy's eyes widened. "You? But you're just his scribe!"

Baruch, son of Neriah, sighed again. "I know that, you know that, and God knows the whole city should know that, but they weren't convinced. Do you want to hear the rest of it now, or should we call it a night?"

The boy burrowed his face into the folded blankets he put under his head for softness, scrunched up his body so that his hands, knees, and toes were touching his father, and said, "Now, now, now!"

Baruch paused to tickle the boy as he acceded to his command. "All right, all right. Where was I? Oh, yes—"

Pasher had quite the day, although you might not have known it just by looking at him. As soon as the men left, he went to his cellar, where he had stored his scrolls to avoid any fire the Babylonians might set, and pulled out the counseling files. He rummaged for a while, never having devised a useful system for finding the one he wanted. A spark lit his face when he came across the Jeremiah scrolls, and he took them upstairs without putting away the others.

The rest of the day would have looked uneventful to an observer. Pasher would spend a while reading, his head often nodding as he recalled a salient point, occasionally stopping to jot down a brief note. For breaks, he would wander over to his pots, scrounging for a nibble to fortify him in his task. Only someone who could get into his mind, or be told what was going on there, could have known that he went to bed that night having fully figured out what he would tell the committee.

Jeremiah's day was more obviously active. Once the committee had left, he ate breakfast, and then sat, eyes closed, breathing at a pace that allowed for deep thought. When he was done, he opened his eyes, uncrossed his legs, stood, and left his house. The rest of the day, he wandered the city, searching and finding the refugees who, months after 5/9, were still not sure they could come out of hiding.

Many of them were so dehydrated as to need transport to the healing centers, to start the slow process of reintroducing liquids and solids in livable amounts. Others could be helped with a bit of food and an encouraging word, while yet others could be directed toward some of the available farming land outside the city. Squatting had become a viable form of ownership, and letting people know of the possibility was taking up any spare energies Jeremiah had.

He dined late that night, his rounds taking longer than usual because of their greater success. Baruch showed up after dinner, their appointed time to review and record the day. Jer spoke of his frustration, his hopes that the prophecy would come soon.

Baruch said, "Master Jeremiah, why worry? There have been longer gaps before, and the Word of God always returned."

He sighed. "The leaders are restive, I can tell. A few more days of silence from the Lord, and who knows what will happen?"

Baruch murmured some comforting words, but they both knew it was futile and not his place, so he said good night and left. In former times, he had been allowed to stay and watch the Master's night-time ritual, the repeating to himself all that had gone right that day, his excising thoughts other than those of God, and his posing a question on which he would hope to receive guidance from the Lord.

Since 5/9, the Master had pulled back. It was not, he had made clear to Baruch, a diminution of his love, it was simply his inability to rouse himself from his concern with the Ruins and the Aftermath. Baruch stopped outside the door to offer a prayer that tonight would be the night, that the answer would come, and that the people would be prepared to hear it.

The next morning, Jer woke up, words of thanks springing to his lips, fifty years of recitation having brought him full circle from conscious to automatic and back to experiencing real gratitude for God having given him another day.

Checking his mouth for any taste of prophecy, he shook his head, turned to the wall and scratched a ninth mark, one for each day of futility since the delegation had come to him.

The boy interrupted. "Dad, that's the same way you said it for when he woke up on the eighth day, and the seventh, and the sixth."

Baruch kissed the mop of hair on top of his head. "Beautiful, very observant. That's because, for Master Jeremiah, every morning he did not get the Word was exactly the same as the one before. Now, do you want to ask more questions, or should I go on?"

The boy settled back, and Baruch picked up his tale.

When the fifty delegates knocked on his door and got word that there had been no Word, the Executive Committee quickly delegated tasks and headed to Pasher's. He was waiting for them, his scrolls again neatly rolled to avoid air damage. This time he ushered them into a back room of the house, which he had formerly called an office. In this room, he still had several hides on which to sit, and he waved the Committee members to them.

When they had arranged themselves, he began, the review of his notes having restored much of his confidence. "Let me remind you at the outset that you have given me quite a task. We have discovered no surefire method for separating true prophets from fakes. Remember that whole Hananiah incident, where he broke the yoke Jer was wearing, where Hananiah said everything was fine and we'd beat the Babylonians, and Jer said no, *and* that Hananiah would die before the year is out, and then he passed on a day *after* the New Year.

176

"I won't even get into the rumors that he ordered his family to delay the announcement of his death so Jer wouldn't get credit for a correct prediction, but you get my point, I hope. Who was right? Was Jer right all along, or did something go bad after Hananiah made his prediction, so that God's plans changed?

"One more caveat that came out of my spending a day with my notes. Remember, as I talk, that Jer and I worked together *years* ago, at the early and midstages of his career. It was when he was a young prophet, trying to cope with the frustrations of his profession. As time went on, as he grew into it, he turned to me less and less. It's been maybe eighteen, nineteen years since we've had any professional contact, and one thing I can tell you with absolute certainty is that people change, no matter how much they think they don't. So all that I'm about to tell you is my best guess, not an absolute certainty. Am I clear?"

Heads nodded and bodies leaned forward, anxious to hear the verdict.

"Here goes. The Jeremiah I knew, all those years ago, was fairly balanced. He had the episodes of prophecy, sure, but they were those of a pessimist tinged with optimism. He still seemed to hold out hope for change, for improvement, and he also still had visions of comfort. And, not to pat myself on the back, his work with me seemed to help him hold on to a multifaceted view of reality. After our sessions, he seemed better able to understand that others saw the world differently than he did, and more ready to try to work with that to bring incremental change for the good."

Pasher paused, drank from the cup of wine, rolled it around his mouth, and then went on. "But a little before he stopped coming to see me, there was a turn for the worse. He started wearing that yoke, as you may

177

remember, as if he were a beast of burden and, oh, I think about the fourth year of Yehoyakim's reign, he began to speak differently as well. I'm not exactly sure how I would characterize it, but back then, I made a notation that there seemed to be a new sense of despair I hadn't seen before, and he spoke more often of surrendering completely to the Babylonians.

"My notes end there, because he broke off our work, never a good sign in a therapeutic situation. It was after that, also, that he began getting into trouble with the law, being thrown into the pit for extended periods of time. Obviously, he would say it was the prejudice of the king's men, but a descent into lawlessness is ordinarily proof of continuing mental health issues. If not for the complicating fact that many of his prophecies seem to have come true."

Another pause stretched on, creating some fidgeting around the circle, but Pasher betrayed no inclination to continue. John prompted him. "So your diagnosis?"

Pasher cleared his throat. "Well, as I said before, I would not call it a diagnosis unless Jer wanted to come in, have a few sessions, and sign a waiver of confidentiality. And also, we in the profession always strive for a full, balanced picture, not some black-and-white determination, so it would be a matter of listing competing tendencies within Jer's personality.

"But I suppose I would say that he has always shown some signs of instability, varying between doom and comfort with a tendency to the negative. It would seem to me the comfort side took a major hit about two decades ago, for reasons we may never know and that he has been struggling with an increasingly depressive worldview ever since."

Jazz couldn't hold back. "But could that be because that was the Truth, the way God was telling him to speak?"

Pasher shook his head, cast his eyes down. "I cannot, of course, say for sure, but in my profession, steady pessimism generally reflects pathology, not health. I would have to say, given his prison record, his failure to stay with a therapeutic regimen, and his overall negativity, that he had some kind of breakdown, around the fourth year of Yehoyakim's reign, from which he has never recovered."

This time, Az broke the silence. "And could Baruch have played a role in this?"

Pasher's head snapped up. "Baruch?"

Az waved his hand, impatient with the pretense at ignorance. "Ben Neriah, the king's servant, who fancies himself the prophet's scribe. Could he have played a role in Jeremiah's mental status?"

Pasher asked, "How long has Baruch been serving Jer in this way?"

"I have no idea."

The therapist looked off into the distance as he pondered. "I'd need further details to be sure, but a person in a precarious state could certainly be easier prey for someone with a particular agenda. Had Baruch gotten it into his head that it was better to make peace with the Babylonians and found himself losing that political battle, it is *conceivable* he might have helped Jer learn to emphasize that side of his own personality as well. I can't say with certainty, but certainly it's conceivable."

The group thanked him and left. At the door, by unspoken unanimous agreement, each walked his own way, what they had heard too momentous to yet allow for discussion.

Jer woke the next morning and did not even bother to taste his mouth. The beatific smile on his face enriched the morning thanks for awakening, put enthusiasm in his washing, praying, and eating. He had expected the knock at the door at least by the time his morning rituals were done, and a hint of impatience crept into his face as he sat and waited after breakfast.

For most of the morning, he held himself in check by thinking up excuses for their tardiness. As the sun rose ever higher, it dawned on him that they had decided not to come. By noon, he was pacing his hovel, considering what to do.

Finally, he summoned them. When the messenger came to John's, bearing the prophet's command to assemble at his house, he and his brother considered ignoring it. Polling the group, though, it became clear that enough of them still had soft spots for the old man that a show of disrespect would backfire. Sighing, he sent word out to the group to meet outside the prophet's, to plan how they would handle this.

When they had assembled, John spoke to them, eyes scanning the crowd for reactions. He spoke of Jeremiah's long service to the nation, noting who made motions of agreement or support. He spoke of how much more secure their lives would be in Egypt, nodding in satisfaction at how many understood that simple truth. He concluded by reminding them of their commitment to listen to whatever the prophet had to say, and smiled at the hesitation he could see on their faces.

He closed, saying, "We have a great deal to consider, and a responsibility to the nation to fulfill our assigned tasks as their representatives. We'll hear Jeremiah out, and I pray to all the gods that they will guide us on how to react."

Their murmurs and shouts of support told him he had performed his role as leader to a T, articulating for them exactly what they all had been thinking. As they neared the prophet's house, people clapped him on the back or shook his hand, thanking him for his leadership and his careful guidance.

The boy was fully asleep, his breath moving in and out in the regular cadence his father knew so well from hours of standing at his door over the years. Not quite asleep enough, though, because he startled when his father moved to get out of bed. Eyes still closed, he said, "No, no, I'm listening, please finish."

Baruch hesitated. "Perhaps tomorrow night; it's late, you're tired, and the story's not going to change if we give it another day."

His eyes had opened, and he sat up. "I'll sleep late tomorrow, I promise, but we've been telling this story for weeks now, and I really want to get to the end. Please?"

"All right, but I have to go a little faster if we're going to finish tonight, okay?"

The boy nodded, and stayed upright to ward off drowsiness.

"Okay, so they get to Jer's door, and he gives them the good news, or at least, what I would have thought was good news, right? He tells them God was done with punishments and would work with them to rebuild, that all they had to do was stay, and plant, and bring the Land back to what it was, and God would help them."

The boy was puzzled. "So, I don't understand. How come we're in Egypt?"

Baruch pointed at him in agreement, and touched the tip of his nose.

"Excellent point, but I don't know if you'll be able to believe the answer, because I'm not sure I do. The group, led by Az and John, told Master Jeremiah he was lying, that God hadn't spoken to him, that *I,* if you can imagine, had put him up to this!"

The boy's eyes widened, his mouth opened. "You? But you're his faithful scribe!"

Baruch laughed, unable to bear the joy in hearing his offspring independently come up with the same words as his father. "I know! It was so crazy! But it didn't matter; they had made their decision. What was worse was their dragging your mother, me, and you with them. So does that answer your question, why it is that we're here if God wants us to have stayed back in the Land?"

The boy shook his head. "That's not what I asked you."

Baruch teased, "Did you mean to say, 'Thanks very much, Dad, for taking three weeks to tell me such a long story and for letting me stay up so late to finish it, but I have more questions still?'"

The boy smiled, looked up at the ceiling and recited, "Thanks very much, Dad, for taking three weeks to tell me such a long story and for letting me stay up so late to finish it, but I have more questions still."

"And what are they?"

"What I really wanted to know was what to say to the other boys at school when they make fun of me for not going to sun worship. I'm sure you don't think I'm going to spend three weeks telling them this whole story."

Baruch blew out a breath, and thought for a minute before answering.

"Really, I think you should tell them nothing."

"Nothing?"

"Yes, nothing. You know, Master Jeremiah tried to talk to them about it, even once they had called him a liar, even once they had brought him here. And you know what they said?"

The boy shook his head, knowing his role in the telling of the tale.

"They said they weren't going to listen to him, that it was only because they *had* listened to him before that all these disasters had happened. Can you imagine?"

The boy shook his head, and yawned. He knew when his father was getting caught up in the stuff the boy couldn't understand yet, and started thinking fondly of sleep. Baruch caught the hint.

"But enough of that. The important thing for you to know is that we must stay faithful to our way, that if we do, even if it's hard, even if the others make fun of us for not worshiping like they do, even if they pick on us, God will reward us. Maybe I won't make it back to our Land, but you will."

The boy pouted. "But it's so hard!"

Baruch was off the bed by now. He leaned down to give his son one last kiss, and said, "I know it is. Don't you think it was for me, too, all those years in the Palace, with all the other advisers telling the king I was a traitor, loyal to the Babylonians and not the Jews? We just have to keep our eyes on what's important and what's real. If we stay faithful, away from the idols and the other foolishness, we will see the reward when the Land is rebuilt."

This time he made it to the door before the boy stopped him with the final question of the night.

"But Dad, how do you *know* that's going to happen?"

The father smiled at his cue. "Because Master Jeremiah said so—"

The boy finished with his father, the words that had become the family motto, "and Master Jeremiah speaks in the name of God."

LAST ONE OUT, TURN OUT THE LIGHTS

Malachi had been preparing for the Interview since barely out of childhood. Back then, enough adults had asked him the question, furious at his calling out their hypocrisies for all to see. They meant it as an insult when they said, "What do you think you are, a prophet?"

Finally, at thirteen, he got the point. As he was then, scrawny and impoverished, they were right to laugh at the thought. But he made it a goal, found a Prophecy Program washout and pestered him into teaching him the exercise routine. Ten years of push-ups, sit-ups, stretches, and runs meant that physical failings would not give them an excuse to reject him.

Nor would money be the issue. The teenage Malachi had kept his eyes in his head, his ears to the financial ground. Seventeen real estate coups later, with a few thousand head of cattle thrown in along the way, he was well-enough off that that too would not be how they excluded him. His having used a fifth of his fortune for feeding the poor and clothing the hungry should ensure he passed entry requirements for character as well.

Scholarship and imagination were the ones that worried him, since the admission committee refused to set well-defined standards. Still, he'd always enjoyed studying and it stayed with him well, and his dream portfolio was at least as thick as anyone's he'd ever seen. Flicking an imaginary speck from his outfit before heading in to meet the examining prophets, Malachi allowed himself a satisfied smile. If anything was certain in this life, it should be that he would be admitted to the Master's Program in Prophecy.

187

Zachariah—"Zach to all my friends," he would say—was similarly unworried, but less happy about it. He had always liked Grandfather Iddo, enjoyed hearing his stories, and relished the games they played together. But the day the old man singled him out as his successor had been the last unpressured one of Zach's life.

Old Pa's stories of the days when he was still getting the Word suddenly carried a new edge. Now, each time he would finish, he would say, "Not that that could happen to me anymore." Then he'd laugh, patting his stomach, "I'm not in that kind of shape."

"But you, Zachariah," and he would lean forward, the kindly grandfather's face changing to one of such focus and intensity that it took all of Zach's considerable will to hold the old man's stare, "now is *your* time, to show us all how far you can go."

His lazy days wandering the countryside, feeling the wind blow through his hair, watching the small animals bound or slither their ways around the hillsides, came to a sudden end, sacrificed on the altar of his grandfather's decree. Strolls became exercises in meditation; hikes morphed into explorations of the meaning of life and the nature of God; where before he might have jogged, now he had to run.

Each trip to the store, Iddo would load his grandson's bags with a little extra, for the physical effort and to test him on how he would choose to distribute it to the city's needy. Casual citations of Scripture turned into tests of intelligence, insight, knowledge, and character. It all guaranteed admission; as if, Zach thought before he walked into the Interview room, the family legacy alone was not guarantee, and burden, enough.

Haggai was the only one of the three sure the Interview would end in rejection. With so few graduates since the Return from Babylon, he knew the Program's administration would not waste scholarship resources on an unproven, unlineaged kid from the hicks. That his teacher had sent him was flattering, and would give him exciting stories for years to come, but his certainty that this was as far as he got freed him from the pressure others were feeling. Whistling with the happiness of one who has nothing to lose, he headed into the Interview room.

It had gone swimmingly for Malachi until this point. Stalling for time, he leaned forward and said to the little man behind the desk, "I'm sorry, could you repeat that?"

The examiner, last in a series, played with the mustache he obviously groomed for long minutes each morning. He lowered his voice yet another octave to stress his superiority, then said, "I said, do you have any questions about the Program?"

Mal shrugged, considered, blew out a deep breath, and said what he was thinking. "There's been talk you're going to close down. Is that true?"

The hands on the other's facial hair paused, surprised, perhaps intrigued, at such forthrightness from a prospective entrant. "Where would you have heard such a thing?"

"I don't know, from people I told I was applying, from strangers who saw me practicing, here and there."

The interviewer smiled, his tone indicating that Mal had much to learn about rumors. "I assure you, we would not take applications if we were thinking of closing. What kind of people do you think we are?"

En route to campus for Induction Day, Zach's thoughts were less on how happy he had made his grandfather than on what to say at the meeting-each-other exercises. Telling the truth would restrict his potential circle of friends to legacies like himself or the climbers who thought he might help them leapfrog the Program's informal social ladder. Omitting the family information—a white lie, he assured himself—would widen the pool of friend-candidates, but backfire worse if he was caught.

"The seal of God is Truth," Grandfather always said. Sometimes the truth hurts, Zach thought.

Huffing as he reached the top of the hill, Haggai entered the Registrar's office and let his satchel of clothing and linens thud in front of the table marked "1Y." The man behind the desk was loud and friendly, sticking out a hand, and saying, "Hi, I'm David, and I'm here to get you set up and moved in. You are?"

He timed the words to each outward pant. "Haggai… from…Beit Guvrin…"

David checked him off and said, "Yep, got you right here. All the First Years are in the new guys' dorm; after a year, you can find your own digs if you want. Out this door, turn left, you'll see a hill. The building on top, ladder to the third floor, that's where you'll be bunking. You can bring your stuff there, then come back here for the rest of the rigmarole."

Haggai stifled a groan as he put his backpack on his shoulder.

"Someone's not quite ready for the physical demands of our little Program, I see." The speaker, taller and built like any trainee's dream, pushed off the wall that had been supporting him and smirked his way over. "A few hills and all out of breath, are we? I'm Shim'i, son of Avneri, so mind you answer with respect."

Haggai's blank look led him to add, "Grand-nephew of Jeremiah, don't you know anything? This whole Program only got reinstituted for people like me, the ones who would certainly graduate. We both know that merit cases like you are for public relations, hmmm? Especially as you haven't even conquered your physical self yet!"

Haggai stifled the stinging response that sprang to his lips. Aside from all else, any points he would have scored would have been lost in the mirth Shim'i and his cohort of friends would mine from Hag's shortness of breath.

The incident hurt more than psychologically, because he decided to avoid Shim'i's section of Physical Conditioning class. Knowing the Program as he did, though, Shim'i had chosen the easier instructor. Haggai found himself struggling with Goliath, called that as much for his roar as for his size.

Goliath not only ran them ragged, he made them chant. Stupid as his ditties were, they burned themselves into Haggai's head, accompanying him for the rest of his life.

Most of them were easy, like "I don't know, but I been told, prophecy makes you mighty old; I may come to the Program as a young man, but I won't leave until I hear from the Man," or "It don't matter if you're a man or not, prophecy comes when God sees what you got; You want to make it into the elite, pay attention when you walk down the street."

It was on the hardest runs that Goliath would pull out a chant Haggai could not understand, draining precious energy. It went, "Don't be thinking you can force God's hand, just leave yourself open to being brought into the band; God doesn't come to those who deserve, the angel visits those who come to serve."

Over months, as he got used to the effort, he was able to still breathe regularly and look around. Only then did

191

he notice that they took one of five morning routes, each passing the Temple Mount. It became a lifeline, knowing that once he reached the Mount, he would make it through that day's run without collapsing.

It was during First Year that the three became friends. Haggai was meditation training along one of the morning jogging routes, enjoying taking the path at a pace that allowed air to move with ease in and out of his lungs. He noticed the more thickly muscled twenty-year-old only as the latter caught him on his right.

As he passed, the newcomer said, "You better pick up the pace, because if Goliath sees me go by you so easily, boy, will you ever get it."

Terror set Haggai off on a brief desperate sprint; he went three lengths of a furrow before he remembered that he was on his own time, free of the dreaded presence. Turning, he saw the other grinning, pleased with himself.

"Very nice, break the best meditation I had all week!"

Intruding on practice was a major Program no-no, calling for immediate contrition. The other trainee said, "I'm sorry, I didn't realize; I thought you were just out walking. Meditation practice, that's rough. And out here in the open, with all these distractions yet? Pretty ambitious. Name's Zach, by the way; well, Zachariah, but I go by Zach."

As they shook hands, Haggai said, "No father to mention, or great-uncle?"

Face clouding over, kicking at a few stones in the road, Zach looked down and said, "Um, well, there is, but we don't need to make an issue out of it, do we?"

"Tell me who it is, and we'll see."

He spoke in a voice so soft, Haggai almost missed the crucial last word. "The whole name is Zachariah, son of Berechyah, son of Iddo."

"Iddo as in…"

"Yeah, the prophet."

Zach saw the fall in Haggai's face, and his voice had a winning desperation as he begged, "No, wait, before you get like that, please don't get like that. I know how the others act; I heard about the Registrar's Office on the first day, but that's not me, I promise. Believe me, it's no picnic coming from my family. If I mess up ever, you should hear how they all go off on me! 'That doesn't seem like the behavior of a prophet, but maybe they've got a new system in the Program these days.' Since I'm twelve, I've been hearing that, or things like it. 'Hmm, would a prophet take an extra piece of cake?' And think about this: if *you* don't graduate, well, making it here was an accomplishment, but if *I* wash out, the hopes of an entire family go down with me."

Malachi arrived for the end of Zach's speech, walking the path in the meditative pose the Program taught. His jaw dropped as he said, "Since you're twelve!? I thought I had gotten a jump by starting at thirteen, and I didn't have any prophet grandfather to show me the way! Hey, Haggai, isn't it? How are we ever going to fill a gap like that?"

Haggai smiled, as he said, "I'm just figuring that if they admitted us, we must have *some* chance. Especially since they're giving me financial aid. But aren't we quite the motley crew: a legacy, a guy who's been working at it for years, and a guy who got lucky by impressing his teacher!"

Their bond eased the years of well-defined coursework. The rhythm of workout, meditation, text study, ritual commandments, acts of kindness, and practice at critiqing current events and social trends left little downtime. When it came, they spent it together, studiously avoiding questions of whether they'd complete and certify.

Their unspoken attempts to wall off their anxieties had to fail at some point. Haggai was flooded by them the day of Shim'i's certification ceremonies. The acid rose in his throat as he watched his former tormentor bow his head to be declared a prophet in Israel. His sincerity when he had publicly apologized two years earlier had not healed the scab on Haggai's psyche, which still reopened at the slightest pull. He spent the ceremony trying to suppress the jealousy bubbling up inside.

Rehashing in the student lounge that night, the other two tried to cheer Haggai by citing the Manual, one of their favorite pastimes, a way to poke fun at themselves and the Program while also reviewing lessons they needed to know. Zach came up with "Anger is counterproductive and a secondary emotion."

The line had come to Haggai that day as well, as he tried to focus elsewhere than on the stage, so he had his retort ready. "Yes, but as Solomon said, there's a time and place for everything. I'm thinking now's the time to be a little angry."

He reached for the wine jug they had been sipping, meaning to down the rest and kick off a wasted night. As it came to his lips, he happened to look out the window, where night fires lit the ruins of the Temple. Struck by the possibility of allowing his rage to burn guilt-free, he excused himself, pleading the need for personal time. He spent much of the night stomping around the unconstructed site, letting his blood boil and simmer, reveling in the rare pleasure of negative feelings he would not have to blame himself for indulging.

The Program had gotten to him enough that he could not keep it up. After a few hours, anger gave way to disappointment and sadness. By then, he had traced all five of Goliath's paths around the city, each time ending at the Ruins, hearing the stones of the Temple call out to him, begging him to take up their cause. When he threw himself into bed, exhausted, he had almost forgotten the name Shim'i, son of Avneri, the Program, the instructors, and even the competition with the other students.

The next day dawned bright and clear. Haggai woke early to clear away the cobwebs of exhaustion before going to watch the ceremonies in honor of the New Moon. He walked slowly, meaning only to calm his feelings, to take the edge off his frustration at the derelict footprint of the Temple.

His anger was gone. Luxuriating in the calm that bathed his being, he went longer than he had intended, and came late to the ceremony. Settling into the first seat he found, he steeled himself for the platitudes about how they longed for the day sacrifices such as these would be offered at a rebuilt Temple.

When he started feeling flushed, he thought it was leftover from his walk. How he got from there to shouting, he never knew. As his voice came out, louder than he had ever heard, he also found himself pushing through the thick crowd, saying, "Thus speaketh the LORD of hosts, saying: This people say: The time is not come, the time that the LORD'S house should be built."

The intimidating authority in the voice, also new, at least saved him from the return elbows he surely would have absorbed under other circumstances. The leaders halted to listen, as Haggai repeated those words until he reached the platform. He came out of it gradually, the

Presence leaving first, and then his muscles slowing from a shake to a quiver to exhaustion. Last, his eyes cleared, and his mind was returned to him.

Apologies for how he had just embarrassed the governor and High Priest, Zerubavel and Yehoshua, came tumbling out of his mouth. "I'm so sorry for interrupting; it just came over me…"

They were having none of it. "Please, Master Prophet, let us not waste time on politenesses. We wish to heed your message, but need to verify its truth. You'll forgive us, but you wear the tunic of a trainee. Have you certified?"

Haggai shook his head. "No, not at all. This was my first time."

They both raised their eyebrows in surprise. Yehoshua continued. "It was most convincing, I assure you. Remarkable, actually. Make sure to write it down, show it your instructors—I'd be happy to vouch for you, if they give you any problems."

Zerubavel had a province to manage. "More important: do you have anything else to say to us?"

Haggai had no idea; he paused, checked himself up and down, then shook his head from side to side. Zerubavel had not reached his stage in life by being satisfied with a negative answer. "Well, with all due respect, and without doubting you, I am not sure I understand what the Lord was saying. Did He really mean we should spend our resources rebuilding the Temple when our crop yields barely feed the populace? When any structure we built would be a pale imitation of the lost one?"

He knew what he had to say, much as he disliked it. "I have no more Word."

Zerubavel and Yehoshua conferred with their eyes, and then the governor said, "Well, again with all due respect, perhaps you could seek further clarification, and let us know more definitely what we are supposed to do. Would three weeks be enough time?"

Haggai was about to admit that a quarter of an hour ago he could not have said six more years would be enough. A new Voice inside told him to say he needed until the twenty-fourth of the month. He spent the way back to campus wondering how he could be sure that he could do again what he did not know how he had done the first time.

His friends' reactions were each surprising. Zach, with so much riding on his own completing, yet exuded unmitigated happiness at his friend's good fortune. Malachi moped, unable to hide how crushing he found it not to have been first. Worse, in the days that followed, he seemed to search for any excuse to distract Haggai. "Hey, wanna grab a beer?"

"Sorry, I can't, I've only got two weeks left."

"You know, you were a lot more fun when you weren't so high on yourself, when you were plain Haggai from the village!"

Without the stress of the deadline, Haggai knew, he would have stayed silent. Instead, he said, "That's not fair! I've got to face the governor, for God's sake, and I can't risk going in there with nothing to say!"

Mal's face suggested a heated response on the horizon, but Zach hushed them both. He turned to Haggai. "C'mon, we're getting out of here."

"Zach, I told you..."

"Not to drink, to train. We'll do it together. Until the twenty-fourth of the month, at least, you and I are going to eat, breathe, and sleep prophecy—we'll run together, meditate together, find people who need help, find

197

problems that need addressing, hypocrisies that need uncovering, working out what people need to hear, what God wants to tell them. I'll tell my wife, you tell yours. Deal?"

Two weeks later, standing at Zerubavel's door, Haggai still had no evidence the crash course had worked. He had woken early to chop wood for the widow down the street, dropped off breakfast for the orphans in the next neighborhood, and spent the morning in silent prayer, hoping at each moment to feel the flood of inspiration. Nothing. He stepped forward, took his last full breath of the next hour, and knocked.

The governor, famed for his formality, surprised Haggai by answering his own door. Yehoshua already sat at the table that took up most of the small room, one chair in the corner inhabited by a man Haggai had never seen before. Zerubavel waved in his direction, introducing him as Seraphiah the Scribe, there to ensure they not lose any of Haggai's words.

Haggai stepped forward, unsure of what was supposed to happen. He sat opposite Yehoshua, and they made desultory small talk, the other two clearly expecting him to pull out the rolls of prophecy he had accumulated over the intervening weeks. Only when Zerubavel brought them around to the unspoken question, tenderly raising the recent famine and economic troubles, did Haggai feel the Presence return, heard his mouth say:

"Is it a time for you yourselves to dwell in your ceiled houses, while this house lieth waste?"

That was nothing new, but it did draw the other two in. Zerubavel spoke first. "Sure, you're right; in an ideal world we would be rebuilding the Temple. But look: with the recent problems, people are barely making ends meet. To embark on a fund-raising drive now, well, we

198

might get the thing up, but there's no way we'd get the money to make the kind of structure God deserves."

Haggai's Voice would not be out-argued, nor swayed by seemingly sensible considerations. It said, "Now therefore thus saith the LORD of hosts: Consider your ways. Ye have sown much, and brought in little, ye eat, but ye have not enough, ye drink, but ye are not filled with drink, ye clothe you, but there is none warm; and he that earneth wages earneth wages for a bag with holes."

Yehoshua stepped in, giving Haggai a chance to breathe. "Are you suggesting our economic distress is related to the Temple's not being built?"

The Word had taken its time coming but was in full throat now. Haggai felt himself shaking as it pushed its way out.

"Go up to the hill country, and bring wood, and build the house; and I will take pleasure in it, and I will be glorified, saith the LORD. Ye looked for much, and, lo, it came to little; and when ye brought it home, I did blow upon it. Why? saith the LORD of hosts. Because of My house that lieth waste, while ye run every man for his own house. Therefore over you the heaven hath kept back, so that there is no dew, and the earth hath kept back her produce. And I called for a drought upon the land, and upon the mountains, and upon the corn, and upon the wine, and upon the oil, and upon that which the ground bringeth forth, and upon men, and upon cattle, and upon all the labor of the hands."

He got back to the student lounge to find Zach waiting, the anxiety written on his face. Haggai clasped his friend on each shoulder, "Omigosh, you would not believe it, Zach, they ate it up! In the budget and everything; they said three months to gather materials, and then it'll get done. ASAP, they told me. Let me

199

just hand the record to the office, and then we're celebrating, on me!"

The smile on the legacy's face receded as he shook his head in a firm no. "I don't think so, mister, we've got work to do."

"What do you mean? I've got more than enough here to graduate. Changing national policy's good for certification, don't you think?"

"Graduate? Is that all you want? Don't you see? You've got the Gift, man! You could make it into the Books! You want to give up now? Unh-uh!"

Once again, Zachariah's instincts paid off. Three weeks later, he had another vision. And, as Zach had bet, it was another home run, good enough not just for graduation but for Inclusion in Scripture. Better for their relationship—worse for Malachi's mood—the training helped Zach, too, as he got his first a little after Haggai's third.

For Mal, matters went further downhill when Haggai had another burst on the twenty-fourth of the ninth month, and Zachariah exploded on the twenty-fourth of the eleventh. The fact of another prophecy would have been bad enough, but its size and length made it worse. Worst of all, though, was Zach's pretending it was anything less than a success.

As he told Malachi, "I figured I'd turn in a little early, I don't really know why. And then, bam, six chapters! And it was some rollercoaster ride too. I mean the start was great, because I had a guide telling me what each one meant. Which reduced *my* anxiety, since Vision Interpretation was my worst class."

Haggai's understanding nods only emphasized to Malachi how far behind he had fallen. "But somewhere along the way, I must have done something wrong, because the guide started expecting me to understand on my own, and I couldn't. When he switched again to just telling me what the visions meant, without checking whether I could do it, I knew I had failed."

Mal grumbled himself to sleep, thinking, *It was bad enough they've so completely outstripped me; did they have to rub it in by pretending to be disappointed with their performance?*

A week later, he was called to meet Jeroab, the next stage in his life's sudden downhill slide, it too brought on by his friends' success. His adviser informed him the Program was probably going to shutter its windows. What with Haggai and Zachariah having launched themselves, he said, some were arguing that it was time to accept the end of an era. The well of prophecy, too many had come to believe, was running dry.

Mal tried to absorb the words, stunned at the about-face. He had asked this exact question several times, and they had always assured him that he had nothing to worry about. The most recent one had been after he had finished coursework and exams.

His adviser at the time, Kehat, son of Yekutiel, had been short, bald, and overweight, but a certified prophet, which should mean his answer would be the truth. Mal had asked gently, trying to avoid the appearance of confrontation.

"I know you can't reveal confidential information, but I wanted to check that there's no news that will affect my progress."

Kehat liked to play with a set of clay jugs he always kept on the desk. The speed of his movements, Malachi had found, offered an accurate gauge of his nervousness. His hands were a blur as he said, "What do you mean?"

"Well, it's been awhile since anyone's graduated, and there were no new candidates this year, and there are rumors…"

The jugs, used to instruct laypeople in how to measure produce for tithing or sacrifice, came in sizes graduated enough that they could be stacked. Weighing his response, the instructor placed the smallest jug in the next larger one, and so on, until they had all disappeared within the biggest measure.

He then reversed the process, building a tower, the *efah* at the bottom, then the *seah*, then the *omer*, then the *kav*, building a rhythm that reverberated in Mal's mind long after their contact ended, *kav, omer, seah, efah, efah, seah, kav, omer*.

When he finally spoke, his care in choosing each word removed any cadence. "I cannot deny that there may have been…conversations about the Program's future. After all, our graduates are not what they once were. Even the instructors who certified, such as myself, received personal visions, nothing of national or even local import. Some have questioned the propriety of taking on new applicants in such an environment.

"Admittedly, we have some promising candidates, but the long-term viability of our Program, or of prophecy in general, is still much in doubt."

Mal waited for him to come around to the question that hovered between them. *Kav, omer, seah, efah, efah, seah, kav, omer.* On the third round, he tired and asked it himself. "And what does this mean for me?"

Kehat startled, breaking his rhythm as if he had forgotten Mal's presence. "I'm sorry, what did you say?"

"I *said*, what does this mean for me? I've finished three years, I've scored Excellents in Cravings Control,

Character Refinement, Acts of Loving-Kindness, and Meditation, passed my Practicals with Distinction; so what does this mean for me?"

Kehat raised his eyebrows as he spoke, his face trying to echo the reassurance of his words. "Well, of *course* I'll stick with you until you either certify or decide to move on. Whatever happens, you will have your chance to succeed."

His pledge had turned out to be only as powerful as the Assigning Prophet, who had transferred Kehat north two years later. He had gone off apologizing, plaintively assuring Mal he would certainly prefer working with him to trying to convince country bumpkins that all sacrifices had to be at the Temple.

At least Jeroab had stuck. A slim, spare man, his well-trimmed beard and perfectly white tunic hinted at the unnerving fussiness that made students dread meeting with him. He had more than once pointed to a stain on a student's clothing to explain why, in his view, that student had yet to certify.

Mal's face squeezed together, eyes squinting into slits, nose wrinkling as if having been assaulted by a foul odor, mouth sour as if he had sucked a lemon. To no good purpose, he said, "But I'm getting closer, I know it!"

Jeroab tried again to explain. "Look, nothing's been decided yet, but you should see our side. With a Program like ours, we can never be sure when it's time to focus our scarce resources elsewhere. What with the Temple finished..."

"Thanks to Haggai and Zachariah," Malachi threw in.

Jeroab ignored the point. "There's the expense of paying it off, running it. Then there are the returnees to settle and retrain—"

"What, five a year?"

Jeroab nodded. "I know it's not much, but we have to teach them a new language, show them the ways of our society. It's no simple matter to pick up your life and move to another country, you know. Then, add a trip or two a year to Babylonia to see if we can raise those numbers...well, there's only so much we can do."

He took a breath before continuing, the hard part still to come. "More important than the money, though, is that there's ample evidence that prophecy's disappearing. It would be upsetting, I understand, but if it's true, there's no point pouring our energies down a useless drain."

Mal knew that if he spoke, his voice would give Jeroab an excuse to remind him that "unbridled emotion is evidence of a student/candidate's failure to develop proper equanimity." He had no need for Handbook citations now, so he sealed his feelings off and trotted out what was becoming his mantra. "What does that mean for me?"

"That's why I started by saying I was worried. You've got the potential, it seems; your assignments have a phrase here and there, a sharp figure of speech, but you never cross over. I've seen you at retreats, and your trances are impressive, but the material you hand in doesn't give any sense of inspiration, least not enough to certify."

"What do I do, then?"

Jeroab rolled his fingers against each other, trying to rid them of imaginary dirt. "I'd tell you if I could, but you know as well as I do there's no Manual for this part. After the coursework, pretty much it's a question of living right, eating well, and seeing what happens. I've seen a few guys who I would have sworn were going to make the jump, but it never happened.

"But I urge you also to start thinking about whether the problem might be outside of you, beyond your control. Like I said, it may be time to concede that God only wanted us to have prophets early in history, that our job now is to show we can do it on our own. If that's the way it is, beating yourself up about it, or sticking with it, would be futile, maybe silly. Gone is gone."

Before Mal could speak, the instructor leaned forward and held up a hand. "You've got a lot to think about, so let me be clear about the questions you need to answer. Talk it over with your wife—"

"I'm not married."

Jeroab sat back and paused, which for him passed as shock. "I did not know that, or I would have raised it long ago. Let us, perhaps, digress. You need to take care of that life task, especially with the failure rate of first marriages."

He raised a hand, forestalling the student's words. "I know, you think a new marriage would be too distracting, take your mind away from your studies too much. A mistake, letting this Program put your life on hold. It's one thing to chase a dream; it's a worse one to chase a dream at the cost of living your real life."

Telling the guys later, the two prophets sympathized in silence. Haggai suggested going out to get some lunch, but Mal demurred. Lunch meant wine, and one cup meant another, and that meant he'd lose the afternoon. The last thing he needed, on the day he heard news like Jeroab's, was to waste time on a simple physical pleasure.

Instead, Zach scrounged up some bread and leftover cheese. Despite how fast the meal went down, the break and influx of calories lifted Mal's mood. He led them in the Grace after Meals, savoring each word as it flourished in his mouth, keeping a close watch against stray thoughts. The series of thanks—for the food, the Torah, and the Land God had given them, and for this city of Jerusalem, newly rebuilt—wiped away the remnants of his sadness. He was ready to get to his chambers to work.

When he had rented the small space after First Year, he had thought of it as functional, for sleeping and eating. A few weeks' struggle with the distractions of the street and the campus had forced him into using it as a meditation spot as well. Years of experimentation—bed to table to food storage bin, table to door to clothing sack, door to chamber pot to water basin—had settled into six distinct routes, depending on the goal of that day's exercise.

Today would be the need-advice-about-the-future circuit, bed to scrolls to dishes to door. Setting his mind on the finding-a-prophecy problem, as he'd come to call it since the end of Exams, he began his meticulous walk.

Five minutes in, when he found himself at the scrolls for the fifth time in what seemed like five breaths, he shook his head to clear it, and clamped down on his legs and their movements. He watched the weight shift forward and to the left as the back right knee bent, leading the heel and other leg off the floor. As it inched forward, the bottom pivoted, bringing the toes in front of the knee rather than behind it. Once the knee straightened, the toes flexed, bringing the heel closer than the toes. When the heel landed, the weight shifted forward and to the right as the foot rolled onto the floor. Moving onto the toes pulled the back knee forward, starting the process again.

Some claimed meditations were to remove all thought, but Mal chose instead to set his mind fully on some mundane issue, like the components of walking, freeing it of its usual enslavement to the inanities of daily life. The longer he could hold that focus, the more productive thoughts he found once he stopped.

His postmeditation parchment was nearly worn through from years of writing and erasing; it was the thoughts that came out there that convinced Mal he could still make it.

Forty times around the course was his limit of productive focus; sometimes he yielded to the temptation to try to stretch it, but ended up losing more than he gained. Reaching the door with his right foot forward, he brought the back knee in line with the forward leg, placed his left foot on the floor next to the right, and straightened to his usual upright position. Closing his eyes, he took five deep breaths to complete the exercise, struggling to avoid wondering what would come out of his quill.

The words started coming before he had finished his third breath: *he who listens to counsel will become wise.* Mal moved to the chair, trying to stifle any analyzing until after all the words had come. If he started thinking, he'd lose whatever inspiration was coming. *The counsel of God will stand forever.*

He stayed at it for an hour, unable to accept that he was getting only one couplet, " *There are many thoughts in the heart of man, and the counsel of God is what will stand; the counsel of God will stand forever, the thoughts of His heart from generation to generation.*" Nice phrases, for sure, and Mal was pleased to see that his mind had linked a verse in Psalms to one in Proverbs, but there was something here he wasn't getting.

Three days of periodic staring convinced him he needed the input of new eyes, so he headed for campus to find Haggai or Zachariah. On the way, he passed the Study Hall he usually rushed by in order to avoid being late. A long-suppressed instinct won out, and he entered to find a group of Levites wrestling with the very verses written on his parchment.

The Program instructors were adamant in speaking of such moments of serendipity, warning students of the absolute necessity of following them to their conclusion, so Malachi settled in.

The Levi who opened the discussion said, "We connect these verses to each other at the close of the Sabbath, as we leave the haven of holiness and are thrust again into the profane world, struggling to keep our lives balanced between the two. These verses remind us that, much as we shape the world around us, God runs all."

The ensuing back and forth was spirited, verging on heated. Someone objected that if so, they ought to construct a fixed form for the post-Sabbath prayer. A third responded that they had too many communal ordinances already, and the room was off on a debate about how and when central bodies should legislate.

Malachi did not have to close his eyes to remember when he, too, had put his faith in study. Even with all his years reaching for a more direct link to Truth, he could still remember all the texts and countertexts, could have jumped into the fray if the spirit had moved him.

The nostalgic smile that came to his face gave him the clarity he sought. It was time, the Voice inside said, for a little less prophecy and a little more study. Borrowing a scroll from an obliging Levi, he sat down and unrolled it.

Three weeks later, he bumped into Zachariah. The prophet grabbed his friend by the shoulders, a smile lighting his face. "Mal! How are you?"

Malachi had known this day would come, was still not sure how to handle it. "I'm good, thanks. Really good, actually. I don't know if you heard, but I washed out."

Zachariah nodded. "I did hear; I was going to call on you, but I didn't know...well, anyway, now that you brought it up, let me disagree. You didn't wash out—they as much as told you they were going to shut you down, and there's more than one person who thinks the whole thing is coming to a close. Getting on with your life seems really healthy to me. But what are you doing? Where are you living?"

He didn't want it to feel this good talking to Zach. "I've gone back to Torah study full time; I certify as a Scribe next week, actually. Yeah, I couldn't believe how fast it went either, but after the first few days, it was like all this information had been waiting to come pouring out, all the lessons I had learned as a kid. So there you have it."

Zach shook his head in admiration. "Wow, I gotta tell you, Mal..."

Now came the next hurdle in introducing his friend to the changes in his life.

"It's Ezra now."

Zach didn't catch it. "Sorry?"

He took another breath. "My name, it's Ezra now. Once I left the Program, the idea of walking around with a name that spoke of my connection to Angels was a little much. Ezra is more comfortable."

Zachariah nodded in understanding. "Who do you intend to help?"

"Huh?"

"Well, if you dumped the name Malachi because it refers to angels, I assume you made a conscious choice when you chose a name that means 'assistance.' Who do you intend to help?"

There was no simple answer, no twenty-five-word summary for how he would direct his life now that it had been set adrift by failure. Stammering, he said, "Oh, well, I guess, I mean, that is, well, uh...anyone, I suppose. Or anyone willing to work with me on their Torah study or practice. Or...well, I don't know yet, really, because I'm busy preparing for exams and for the move to Babylon. What? Oh, yeah, I got a fellowship for post-certification studies. You know, I hear that they are so desperate for scribes you can spend your whole day studying and writing, and then at night they come to you after work, by the dozens, to hear what you've learned that day!"

Zachariah clapped his friend on the shoulder. "It is so wonderful to hear you talking like this; it's the first time in a while you've sounded excited. The last couple of years in the Program, you were doing the work, but it seemed to me, anyway, that your heart wasn't in it. But now...it's like the old Malachi is back, the guy I met in First Year."

Ezra ducked his head, then looked up. "I guess finding your place in life will do that for you. And, besides," he paused for effect, "I got engaged."

"Engaged, you! Unbelievable! What about all your talk about how so many marriages break up, about not wanting to cause that kind of distress to another person?"

Ezra bobbed his head, having asked himself the same before agreeing to the match. "I know, I know, and it's not like I'm not worried. But I came to realize that everyone out there isn't me, and my marriage will be my responsibility to keep together. I'm sending out the invitations next week; it'll probably be the last blowout before we bury the Program forever!"

When they met again three years later, the change in their fortunes startled at least one of them. The assistant at Ezra's side, guiding his rush from lecture to rally to campaign stop, triaging the spurts of people approaching to ask for help, followed his eyes as he saw Zach meandering down the street, meditating on his movements. The assistant started to ask what was so interesting about this man, but Ezra hushed him and approached. The faraway look in the prophet's eye made him rue having interrupted.

He apologized. "Pardon me, but I haven't seen you since—"

His voice sucked Zachariah back to reality. The prophet's eyes swam into focus as if rising up from a great depth, the actual world coalescing before him as he processed the words coming out of his old friend's mouth. The process pained Zach, as Ezra could see. Embarrassed, he apologized again, turned to walk away.

Once called, Zach was not so easily dismissed. He clasped his friend's shoulder, turning and folding him into an embrace. His affable smile almost made Ezra believe that whatever he had been pondering could wait.

"Malachi! No, wait, sorry, I mean Ezra! I heard about your return, about the multitude you brought with you. I meant to come see you, but what with my retreat..."

"I heard! What's that all about? My memories were that the Program encouraged being among people!"

"And if it was still around, maybe I'd follow the Manual. But since the Program's gone and I'm still here trying, at some point you have to say to yourself that if what you've been doing didn't work, maybe it's time to try something else."

Of all the changes in his friend, it was Zachariah's eyes that shocked Ezra most. The prophet was clearly aware and involved in the conversation, but the eyes stayed vague and distant, trying to both look far away and focus on what was in front of him at the same time. Zach must have sensed what he looked like, because he shook himself fully out of it, smiled, and said, "Sorry, I didn't mean to babble. It's just been too long since I've spoken to anyone who might know what I'm going through..."

Ezra frowned. "Going through?"

He started to speak, paused, switched gears. "You know what, I'd love to tell you, but I want Haggai there too. Can we maybe meet for lunch, tomorrow, Shira's Inn?"

They made the date, and Zach ambled off, pace and movements suggesting he had sailed right back into his meditation. Before Ezra could assimilate what he had just seen, a man accosted him wanting the Scribe to know *exactly* how he felt about his initiative to compel divorcing their non-Israelite wives.

Ironic if you think about it, Ezra mused. All those years I resisted getting married because of the divorce rate, and now here I am pushing for more of it! The Ways of the Lord are indeed wondrous.

Haggai and Zachariah had already taken a table when Ezra got there. They hugged, held each other at arm's length to examine the ravages of time. Haggai spoke first. "Such changes in our little Malachi. From aspiring prophet to bearer of the Emperor's letter of approval!

Who would have thought you'd trade the certification you didn't get for such august other ones?"

Ezra would have responded in kind and tone if he hadn't been busy trying to not say something thoughtless. It was not that Haggai had let himself go; the strength, physical and moral, still shone forth. But the signs of decay were there, more advanced than Ezra would have imagined.

Like the eyes. Aside from the rings of exhaustion, there was a haunted quality, as if their owner were constantly running himself ragged trying to catch something. Sweeping it under his mental carpet for later, he answered Haggai. "Right time, right place, I guess. When I got to Bavel, the Jews were waiting for someone to call them to dramatic action, and the king was looking for someone to appoint. There wasn't much competition, because all the would-be leaders were way too comfortable to uproot. So I wouldn't be too impressed."

The waiter showed up at that point, and they asked for eggs, pita, and oil, and ordered the house specials. As Haggai quizzed Ezra, the questions were sharp and insightful as ever, but the bloodshot eyes and determined approach to the jug of wine told a more complex story. He would take a mouthful, swish it around his mouth, swallow it, and then pause, as if to check his sobriety each time.

Throughout the two jugs he drank with lunch, he coached Ezra into telling his life story from the wedding on. Finally Haggai paused, and Ezra decided to turn the tables, if only to forestall any more probing. "But what about you? One prophecy from the two of you in all these years?"

For the first time, the wine slurred Haggai's words. "Sadly, I have been forced to consider whether the

213

administrators of the Program were correct. In the best of times, the Lord's ways are inscrutable, but now all the more so. Look at me, for example."

He took another long pull at the jug, and when he looked up the glint of the light off his eyes hinted at moisture. "We already weren't seeing much of each other when I had my last two about how keeping the laws of the Torah would mean a good financial and political future for everyone. Those priests're quite a piece of work, by the way; I'd do my best to stay away from them, if I were you."

The pain emanating from the worn eyes, the worry lines in his forehead, the droop of his head and shoulders almost made Ezra feel relieved that he had never certified. To be at the top and then have it taken away apparently was in fact worse than never having prophesied at all.

Haggai emptied the jug, which opened his mouth again. "I try to get used to having been a flash in the pan, streaking too fast across the sky. But then I look at Zach's last few prophecies, and I can't let it go."

Ezra was puzzled. "Zach's last what?"

Haggai pointed, yielding the floor to him and his tale. Zachariah nodded as he began, as if he had known the conversation would work its way to this. "Two years after my first bunch, almost to the day, I realized it was all over. Because that day, I had the longest one anyone could remember hearing about."

He shook his head at the memory. "And it wasn't like I was trying harder or differently; it felt more like there was a message that needed to get out there, and I had been chosen to do it. No more guide, no more questions, no more symbols. Nope, this time it was words and images, but not that took any interpreting, you know? When I came out of it, I knew exactly what I was supposed to write, even though I couldn't follow all of it myself. Some of it was weird, like a future I couldn't even picture, let alone understand.

"He doesn't agree now, but when I showed it to Hag, he was the first to say it sounded like a farewell to prophecy, a last set of messages for a long time, maybe until the End."

Zach continued as Haggai's shoulders tensed, his head involuntarily moving from side to side in disagreement. "Course now, he's changed his mind, so he tortures himself trying to find more. You know how when you've committed so strongly to something, you can't give it up even when it's time to give it up? That's our friend Haggai. So he wakes up every morning, tries for a few hours, gets frustrated by lunch, consoles himself with wine," he paused to point at the empties in front of Haggai's plate, "and then complains about how he can't get his work done."

Haggai leaned forward, putting a finger up for each part of the other's description of events that needed correcting. "First, I freely admit that I thought your prophecies were the end of it, and I concede I had a hard time accepting that fact. I mean, what would I do with the rest of my life if I'd peaked at thirty?"

He stopped, braced himself, then stuck up his next finger. "Second, Zach didn't mention that he, too, has come to think maybe something more is out there. Did you notice that *he's* drinking milk with lunch? I bet he still tries, morning, afternoon, and night, which tells you he's not so convinced that the era of prophecy is over."

Haggai's tone was edging from the calm of the debater to the anger of an argument. "And third, don't make snide comments about my drinking; it's not like you're bursting forth with the Word yourself."

This was well-traveled ground for the two of them, Ezra could tell. He turned to Zachariah, who seemed less emotionally invested. "Just curious, and meaning no disrespect, since I never certified, so I'm not one to point fingers or anything, and not wanting to offend you…"

Zachariah stopped him. "Ezra, please. You think I don't remember that it's us, Mal and Zach? Ask what you want."

"Well, I'm wondering why you're both so set in your positions. Isn't there a middle ground?"

That caught Haggai's attention. "Middle ground?"

"Yes. What if you're right that there's some piece missing?"

Haggai didn't see where he was going. "But?"

"But it's not for either of you."

Now neither understood. He tried again. "Isn't it possible *your* time was up, but not someone else's? That you'd done your jobs and were released to live your lives?"

They looked at each other, not knowing which should show him the elementary error in his reasoning. Zachariah tried. "But Mal, if it's not one of us, who would it be? Shim'i and that group? Hah! They took their certification, parlayed it into lucrative speaking gigs, and went off to their comfortable lives. You think the Lord's going to visit them with the final Words to guide His people through the rest of history?"

He stopped, and Haggai picked up. "The thing is, Ezra, that—without meaning to sound stuck-up—we're the only two left. The Program's closed, right? Any other graduates out there have given up, because prophecy's over. Leaving me and Zach."

He let the words sit between them, shrugged his shoulders, took the last piece of bread, wiped it in the oil, put it into his mouth with a flourish, and held up his empty hands, palms up in front of him as he lifted his eyes, a gesture that made clear he was done with the conversation.

The meal and conversation concluded, they said Grace. Their good-byes included the meaningless promise to do this again, a social custom so ingrained even those dedicated to discovering the Truth could not avoid falling into the lie.

Ezra stayed after the other two, assimilating what they had told him. When the waiters begged him to let them earn their living, he walked the city, the first contemplative stroll he'd had time for since washing out. Now, when he was out and about, it was to notice and greet the people in the street, to develop, as much as one man could, an ongoing relationship with each. Keeping them all straight in his head, he mused, had been quite the adjustment from trying to empty his mind to let inspiration in.

The retraining, hard as it had been, had paid off. He wouldn't have gotten to know the king unless he had made it on the party circuit back in Bavel. And from there, gaining the king's support in bringing a new contingent of settlers, in strengthening the populace living here. Still, lunch reminded him of the path he had had to relinquish, the priorities he had subscribed to for so many years. His accomplishments had been bought at the price of abandoning the dreams of his youth, his first love.

To shut off the meandering down Regrets Lane, he followed his feet to the Mount; seeing others and the failings for which they came to atone always cheered him up. Keeping his breath smooth, a point of pride as he climbed the steep hill, he approached a woman. "What a pretty lamb! May I ask where you got it?"

"Why, thank you! We got her in town; there was a market with a special on Temple-bound animals. The man was so nice!!! He had been asking five shekels, but when I explained that my family had come all the way from Galilee to celebrate having survived that big flood—you remember, when the rivers overflowed and a few towns were washed away? Well, our house, you would not believe this, was fine! So I just said to Herb, that's my husband, Herb. Herb, come over here and say hi to this nice young man! He was asking me about our lamb, so of course I had to tell him about the flood, and how we're bringing it to celebrate."

Herb had sleepy-lidded eyes and reacted to his wife in slow motion, a haze that Ezra guessed was self-induced, to protect him from her barrages. Herb stuck out his hand. "Hi, Herb, son of Joseph, nice to meet you."

"Anyway, so I was saying, when he first asked for five shekels, I turned to Herb and said, 'Herb, do we have five shekels for the lamb?' Remember that, Herb?"

Herb wanted to be walking, not talking. "Yeah, I remember."

"And Herb says, like I trained him, 'No, dear, we didn't bring that much. We agreed we'd only spend two shekels, so that's all I brought.' Herb can be so convincing at putting his foot down, right, Herb?"

The speed of her mouth was inversely related to the pace of her legs. "Oh, good idea, Herb, I'll catch up with you in a minute. So anyway, I said to the man, 'You heard

Herb, there's nothing to do when his mind is set like that.' He thinks, says, 'Two shekels? Wait here a minute,' and comes back with that beautiful lamb! Can you believe it?"

Ezra couldn't, actually. "Did he tell you why it was cheaper?"

"Oh, he said something about it being blind, but I said to Herb, 'Herb, we're going to be killing and eating the poor thing anyway; who cares if it can see?' And the man agreed, so here we are. We're having a big blowout tonight. Why don't you come?"

There was a time, he knew, when he would have told her that blindness disqualifies a sacrifice. If there was a chance she'd go back, he might still have said something.

It had been one of the sticking points back in the Program, when he was trying to fulfill his Citing Texts requirement. He would say, "Hi, I'm Malachi, a student prophet, and I have to share some verses from Scripture with random people on the street. Would you mind giving me a moment of your time?"

He'd almost washed out then, when it turned out he unerringly found the text that named each listener's most glaring flaw. To save him from further physical abuse, the instructors finally let him cite texts to them, although they too bristled when he could only think of texts that spoke of prophets' failings. His mind would never find verses of comfort; his time in Bavel had at least taught him to accept that aspect of himself.

The priests were the opposite; they were remarkable at that. All smiles all the time, always accepting, whatever you wanted to do was fine, we're happy to have you here, don't worry about it, it's the effort that counts. With competition like that, no wonder the prophets had had trouble getting their message across. Look at him; even *with* the king's imprimatur, it was taking all his skill and effort to stop the intermarriages. It would probably mean that all the rest of the problems would get ignored.

The thought ate at him the whole way to the Mount, the whole hour he watched the closing of the day with the offering of the afternoon sacrifice, the whole walk home. Hearing the door open, his daughter crawled to greet him as fast as she could, followed by his wife's smiling face. He bent over to pick up the one-year-old and stood. When his wife saw his eye, her hand went to her mouth, too stunned to ask.

"I opened my mouth once too often, is all. It's not a big deal; it's only pain."

"But what did you say?"

"Oh, it was my fault, totally. I went to the Temple to watch, you know how I like to do that, and I'd left my assistant home, so people did not recognize me. Well, there's this guy offering a lamb with one ear missing. And it was the third time that day I'd seen something like that, but it wasn't like this was a small blemish, it was a *missing limb*. So, politely—"

"Ezra!!!"

"No, I swear, I was gentle, I promise. I simply mentioned, apologetically, that I had heard that some authorities thought such an animal couldn't be offered."

By now, she knew where the story was going. "And he hit you?"

Ezra shook his head. "No, he took me seriously, made a nasty comment to the priest who'd been about to offer it on the altar, and went to buy a new one."

"Your eye?"

"Oh, the priest was annoyed, because the guy would never trust *him* again."

"And he hit you?"

"No, no, he'd have had to leave the Mount for the rest of the day, lose all that business. No, he was way smarter; he told the next guy in line he wouldn't be able to continue with his sacrifice until I'd been taken care of, and *that* guy did it."

She shook her head, went to the kitchen, dipped a rag in the cold water barrel, and came back out to put it on his face. "Oh, Ezra. Why do you do this to yourself?"

Over dinner, the most interesting news came from the river, where she had done the laundry with the other women.

"Did you hear that Simeon the Scribe sent his wife away? After all those years, too. And took up with one of those non-Jewish ones."

"No!"

"Oh, yes, said he'd had enough; it was the third time that week she had burned the soup, she might as well git, it was time for him to find a woman who cared about making him happy. A Perizite, gorgeous, of course. Can you believe such a thing?"

He closed his eyes for a moment. "Unfortunately, I can; it's the times, they get to you. When everyone else does it, it becomes hard to resist."

She narrowed her eyes. "Are you trying to warn me of something?"

He smiled, the teasing a sign of the security they felt with each other. "The altar would have to shed tears before I'd let a prize like you go, dearest."

After dinner, with the baby in bed and she finishing the day's cleaning, he spent a candle poring over Scripture. Approaching his scrolls area, the usual feeling of peace washed over him. He was well, his wife was well, he was contributing to the rebuilding of a Jewish society...what more could a man truly want?

As if in response, one word jumped out at him no matter what scroll he took out. By the fifth time he pulled a random scroll and found the same word, Ezra—no, Malachi—felt hope stirring. The word was "load," that was how the prophets described it. Not a privilege, not a degree, not a burden. A load, from Sinai, to be released at the time and place assigned. Sitting down, trembling a bit, he let himself hear the small Voice he'd avoided these past years. *Write what you know.*

Closing his eyes, he sat for almost the whole of the candle's life, a faint shaking of his bones the only visible movement. When he opened them again, the smile on his face was that of a captive released. Haggai had been right, as had Zachariah, as had he. There was one more piece out there, but it was not for either of them.

Taking up a piece of parchment, not even thinking about how he would certify, Malachi began to write.

DOOMSDAY METEOR IS COMING: THE STORY OF EVERYPROPHET

Maurice stewed as the people around him blabbered on, ignoring the obvious. All the other stories they had critiqued had been transparent, easy to figure out, but Paul O'Melvaine's was a mystery, and the key was the title, it had to be. Etiquette be damned, he wasn't sitting around for another half hour of this workshop until it was his turn to share his thoughts. He waved his hand, so the instructor could not ignore him.

Bert Parker, the young novelist who made it clear he was doing this for the few bucks he needed until the world recognized his talents, sighed his impatience. Tall, he cut his black hair short enough to be spiky without gel, an unfortunate choice considering the thirty extra pounds he carried. Bearlike also in the slowness of his thought and gesture, Parker added to the impression by dispensing crushing hugs when he was happy with a student's performance.

When he wasn't, he would crush in other ways. "Maurice, were you thinking you absolutely had to interrupt?"

Maurice looked over at the woman who had been speaking. Her carriage spoke of her acute awareness of her impact on the men she encountered, her concern that it might not be as great as it had been twenty years earlier. Vassar or Bryn Mawr, Maurice guessed, clothing, jewelry, and car all saying she had landed the doctor, lawyer, or Indian chief for whom her looks and education had groomed her.

225

"Sorry, Melinda, I know how rude this is, but…"

Grace demanded that a woman of her breeding and social status forgive him, so of course she did, gracefully. "Oh, no, no, it's no problem, go ahead."

Looking at the faces around the eight two-person tables pushed together into a square, it was only now that Maurice bothered to notice he had again disrupted in exactly the way the workshop administrator had warned about in his letter. A flush came to his cheeks as he asked Paul, "What kind of cliché title is *Doomsday Meteor Is Coming* anyway?"

The hush that greeted his question could not have been louder if Maurice had gone skinny dipping in the middle of a black-tie cocktail party by the pool. Knowing he would spend the night kicking himself, he yet could not stop, and opened his mouth to press the issue.

Bert held up a hand. "I was kind of wondering about the title myself, but I think that's the kind of comment that can wait its turn."

Melinda flashed a smile, teeth a few shades whiter than nature could possibly have granted her. "Maurice's point helps mine, actually. I didn't focus on the title, but now that you mention it, it is kind of trite. Which might explain why I felt so disconnected from the story as I read it. I mean, for almost all of it, the characters are going about their ordinary business, one person being rude, another getting annoyed, another making peace between them. If there's a meteor coming, shouldn't somebody be *doing* something? Or at least shouldn't we see some urgency somewhere?"

Paul moved his head and hands as if to respond, but noted Bert's cautioning hand motion and sat back.

Melinda went on, "Also, I guess, I would say your main character seems too passive, you know what I mean?"

Bert shook his head, said, "No, actually, could you be a little more specific?"

She waved her hand, dismissing herself. "Well, like I said, I'm sure I don't know how these things work, and maybe I'm off base…" A few groans escaped from around the table; her habitual apologies before sharing a thought already wore on them in the workshop's third week; they would surely be intolerable by the tenth, "but as your hero reviews the letters he's gotten, each one dumps on him, shows him to be a failure, one after the other."

Angela Franklin's mixed descent had served her well, letting her carry her twenty excess pounds in places that made her look voluptuous rather than fat. She nodded her head as she popped in, her beauty excusing her from the disdain that greeted Maurice's interruptions.

"I know exactly what Melinda means. When I was reading the story, I was also thinking that if I had spent ten years studying the brain waves of religious people, and all along my adviser had been telling me I was going to revolutionize the psychology of religion, and then after all that, the bastard told me I was too far ahead of the field to get a job, I'd have gone postal on him. But Sol, your character? He's so relaxed, I nearly wanted to step into the story and slap him upside his head to wake him up."

The computer geek across from Maurice, whose car and clothing said he had been smart enough to sell before the Internet bubble burst, said to Angela, "So I guess Paul wrote a character who got you emotionally involved in the story, right?"

The laughter ended when Stephanie Mills, long of body and nose, hoop earrings hanging down to the orange-hued dashiki that matched the color of this month's hair dye, opened her mouth. Anticipating the catfight she habitually launched, all five male torsos eased forward to catch the action.

"Sorry to pop in out of turn, but as chair of the Women's Studies Department at the U., I've sat on numerous dissertation committees, and that kind of thing happens all the time."

Melinda's eyes fluttered, and Maurice marveled at her ability to turn the retort that sprang to her lips into such a minimal gesture. The self-control required by etiquette was apparently close to absolute. Whatever she might have wanted to say, she kept her tone mild as she noted that she might be out of touch with the pettiness of universities, but Paul ought to keep readers like her in mind when he considered whether Sol came off as likeable or as a sap.

Stephanie backtracked, as if agreeing with Melinda could ease the sting of her previous interruption. "Absolutely; I felt the same way with the next letter, where Sol finally publishes an article, the one analyzing why some religious leaders—rabbis, imams, priests, and pastors—had so much more impact than others. But the story has it as his *fifty-seventh* article, and I was wondering how he could possibly take all those rejections and plug away. Wouldn't you, Paul, want us to understand why he didn't throw in the towel and get on with his life?

"More important, by *then*, I was getting as antsy as Maurice. As a reader I give you a little leeway, and you've couched the journey with scenes, so you're keeping my attention, but we're over a third gone, and there's no meteor anywhere on the horizon. Are we supposed to be thinking it's literal or metaphorical, or what?"

We're over a third gone, and there's no meteor anywhere on the horizon. Her words completed the circuit that had been trying to close in Maurice's brain since he had first read the submission. He had Googled Paul, his standard practice for his fellow aspiring writers, but found nothing useful. The anxiety on Paul's face as his story got picked apart, along with Stephanie's offhand comment, confirmed to Maurice that he was missing *something*, something Paul thought was important.

Thanking the gods he always kept his laptop open during class, he risked connecting to the Web. The answer had to be in one of the dozens of articles Paul had deposited in various sites online. When Maurice had first found them, he had dismissed them as a quirk; few people were so desperate to get their thoughts out there as to cajole fifty different sites to host an article.

The titles of a few of them had stuck, though, helping him now. He looked up to check that there was still time until his turn. As long as he glanced at whoever was speaking every couple of seconds and nodded as if he were absorbing his or her words, they would think he was taking notes.

Tapping at the keyboard in the modified hunt-and-peck he had perfected, he spelled out Paul O'Melvaine, then hit Enter. The ad popped up, "Did you go to high school with Paul O'Melvaine?" *Blah, blah, blah, where were the articles?* Scrolling through all the Paul O'Melvaines, the ticking of the clock weighing on his patience, he was about to give up when one title caught his attention.

He clicked on the link, www.nerofiddles.com, that was one of them, he remembered. *Waiting, waiting, waiting, why was the damn connection so slow?!* It was the first time he had ever hoped Jack Ash, the used car salesman who saw the natural fit between his professional talents and fiction writing, would speak longer. Maurice gave him the most encouraging nod he knew, confident that Jack didn't need much to keep him going.

The site opened by filling his screen with his favorite ad for Miller Lite. Checking his computer was on "mute" and how many people there were before he'd have to speak, he let himself enjoy the parade of shapely women carrying a case of beer to the beach, rippled men trailing in their wake. He loved the gag, the women putting down their load, stripping to their bikini bottoms and jumping in the water, only to turn and see the men too engrossed in the beer to notice.

Smiling inside, he resisted the temptation to replay and freeze-frame it as each woman removed her top. Getting back to the site's archives, he couldn't find Paul's article. Frustrated, Maurice hit the Back button on the browser, stabbing at it twice to avoid the ad.

Paul *J.* O'Melvaine, that's what he had gotten wrong. *Stupid internal search engine.* There it was, "The Nero Syndrome: Would We Know When Rome Was Burning?" All right, he thought, Paul has the ability to come up with interesting titles, so he chose *Doomsday* on purpose, not because of a lack of inspiration. Where was the abstract?

As he scrolled down, half an ear on whether the woman to his right had begun speaking, the article's section headings lodged in his brain. *Our Amazing Obliviousness to Approaching Disasters: Pompeii, Pearl Harbor, Hiroshima, and 9/11.* Cursing the machine to move faster, he finally got to *Conclusion: The Necessity of Better Predictors for Upcoming Disasters.*

Maurice could feel it coming together, but too slowly. Ten years ago, Paul O'Melvaine, now the author of "Doomsday Meteor is Coming," had written an essay expressing the urgency of finding better ways of predicting calamities. Why put it on a Web site no one ever heard of?

Maureen had started, fingering the small gold cross on her neck, flashing her engaging, off-center smile to take some of the edge off her words.

She said, "First, let me just say that I *really* liked how you mixed different kinds of writing into the story— letters, people speaking, thoughts, Web sites, whatever. I liked the end too, thought it was worth waiting for.

"But, and I'm sorry to maybe pile on, some of the steps along the way need fixing. Take the March 23, 1998, letter, for example. Here, I'll read the part I mean:

Hey buddy, long time! Thanks for sending me "How Religious Transformations Can Affect Global Warming." Took me back to grad school, all those deep discussions over beers at the Village Idiot. It's wild stuff (you seen your shrink lately?), trying to make a scientific case for the claim that our religiosity, or lack of it, affects the earth's temperature.

Like this line: "The evidence thus shows that how people relate to God plays a role in various natural phenomena, not least among them global warming and the enlarging and shrinking of the gap in the ozone layer." That's you in a nutshell, smart, provocative, way out there; if it were up to me, I might have even put it in the magazine, let it stir the pot.

Unfortunately, *Ecology Today* is an advocacy journal, and others here worried that you would make the whole thing seem like a crackpot idea. But thanks for thinking of us, and let's stay in touch,

Jean-Paul

Maureen paused, twirling the cross as she thought about how to phrase her objection. "Don't get me wrong, the letter's well written and all that. Problem is I don't buy it, in two ways. First, I consider myself pretty religious, but come on, how many people do you know—or put it

231

this way, how many people who read—could believe that whether I go to Mass affects the physical universe!?

"Worse, you don't give us any reason to understand how *Sol*, a brilliant guy, a PhD in psychology, would come to such a far-out view! Maybe we need some more *scenes*, showing us how and when he got whacked out on religion. I assume that's what you were trying to get the reader to realize at this point, that he's jumped off the deep end. But I need to see how it happened—did his wife die? A child? A war? You know what I mean?"

She was finishing, Maurice knew, but her comment had given him a better way to find what he was looking for. It took four frantic tries, but "Religion, disaster, O'Melvaine" got him to another Paul J. O'Melvaine article, at www.freudiansunite.com, titled "Are All Dreams Freudian? Possible Prophecies in Our Nighttime Visions."

Bringing it up onscreen, he almost laughed in relief when it opened with an abstract at the front.

> The author claims that scientific dream interpretation errs by restricting itself to the personal and psychological. Gathering a critical mass of anecdotes, the article argues that mainstream science has been overhasty in rejecting the possibility that some dreams contain prophetic elements.

The site had a hit history for each article, and this one hadn't been touched for three years. With the pieces percolating in his mind, Maurice sensed Maureen finishing with one more apologetic smile and twirl of the crucifix.

Desperate to give his mind a chance to work, he noticed how low Paul had slumped, like each critique was banging nails in a coffin. The straight-backed aristocrat had given way to a hunched, defeated old man. A few words of encouragement would do the old boy good.

"Look, Paul, I'm sitting here listening, and I think you might miss a lot of the good points that people have mentioned about this story. It's a readable story, so it wasn't like it was a chore getting through it or anything. And I liked following his life, finding out how hard it had been for him professionally, how he's struggled to get people to listen to the important things he feels he needs to say. And, crucial, I like *him*; I like his pluck, sticking with his dissertation, his plugging away to get stuff published, churning out articles despite the rejections, putting them on Web sites when no ordinary journals would take them."

No reaction from Paul, as if encouragement did not interest him. "But I agree that you might want to rework his specific submissions. Like the last letter, rejecting his piece on, what did he call it, 'the predictive powers of the Bible.' It sounds cool, combining Old Testament prophecies with a regression analysis of the trajectories of previous meteors. I liked the idea of putting them together to argue that an undetected meteor was out there, that it would soon hit Earth with enough size and force to kill 90 percent of the world's population, and plunge the survivors back to pre-industrial times.

"But then you lost me when you had Sol be so tone deaf as to think *Scientific American* would publish such a thing, especially when he's *also* claimed that the odds of survival would jump if a person sincerely worshiped a Judeo-Christian-Moslem God. I'm pretty sure that kind of faith went out of style years ago, and he would need lots better evidence than you have him showing if he's going to bring it back. When I first read it, I thought you were trying to get us to see how his frustration drove him insane, but the way you go in the last few pages seemed to me to mean you were playing it seriously. In which case, it wasn't devcloped enough to be convincing."

The others were agreeing with him, a pleasant change from their usual reaction to his ideas, but Maurice was too busy to notice, his mind groping toward…what? Didn't matter, Bert was summing up, happy to end a few minutes early. *Probably had a warm girlfriend to get home to.*

"I guess we've heard general agreement as to the quality of your structure and presentation. No one said it was hard to get through, we heard no complaints about the characters, no grammar issues I could see. But I'm also hearing worries about realism, which I want to underline. Too much of what you have here contradicts what your target readers know of the world.

"Maybe you could rewrite it using issues at least *some* people accept, even if scientists don't. Like, what if Sol was interested in Eastern medicine, or meditation, or something like that? Or, if that's too trendy, what about Native American rain dances? Anyway, food for thought as you redo it. Do you have any questions for us?"

As he pulled himself up from the depths of the chair, Paul reminded Maurice of a boxer, bloodied and battered, coming out for the last round, a soldier rallying his energies for a doomed storming of the ramparts. He spoke a word at a time, considering each before letting it out of his mouth. "I guess what I wonder is, let's say I was stubborn about having *these* ideas in the story, for whatever reason. Is there a way to get it read?"

Bert wasn't supposed to be negative, Maurice was sure. It would explain the look on his face as he answered. "Um, I guess, well, if your audience is educated, used to the scientific frame of thinking, it's tough. You could try religious journals, maybe science fiction or fantasy, or maybe rewrite it in an alternate universe where everybody already understands that the physical is intertwined with the metaphysical. But in *our* world, I can't see it. Anybody else have anything to say?

"Okay, that wraps up this week; next week we've got the stories Stephanie and Brian gave in today, and we'll expect submissions from…Maurice and Maureen. Hey, two people with the nickname Mo, cool. Okay, have a good week, people!"

The room emptied in its usual rush, the after-class chatter and calls to go clubbing flying by Maurice as he tried to catch the thought flitting around his brain. Paul rose, twenty of his seventy-five years having come into his face in the past half hour. As he passed, he recognized the article on the screen before Maurice could close it or navigate away. He paused, the beginnings of a smile playing at his mouth, putting some twinkle in his moist eyes, "Interesting reading?"

His "no" was slow, some part of Maurice refusing to admit to being too obtuse to figure out the puzzle whose pieces, he felt sure, were sitting in front of him. "I'm sorry to say, I didn't get a chance to read all of it, and I didn't understand it, but it feels like it has something to do with your story, right?"

The other man thought, weighing what he wanted to say. No, not wanted, Maurice decided, the man in front of him was trying to figure out what he was *allowed* to say. *Allowed? By whom?* Too late, he was talking.

"You're an actuary, I think you told us, right?" Paul didn't wait for a confirming nod, the question having been a conversation starter, not a request for information. "In your job, you try to predict the future based on the past, right?" Another unneeded nod. "But you only work with averages; you can't predict the outcome in any *particular* case, right?" Maurice wondered whether he was meant to answer at all, his nods having so little effect on the soliloquy.

Paul was gaining energy as he spoke, getting more animated, moving his hands, pointing, tracing circles, pictorializing what he said as it came out of his mouth. "What if you found a way to predict better, to not only be more accurate, but also more precise, to know not only *when* events would happen, but to *whom*? And I don't mean in a general sense; I mean to look at a person and say, 'you'll be okay,' and at someone else and say, 'you'd better run'?"

"It would revolutionize the world of insurance."

The other man snorted. "It would end it, more like, since everyone would know who was going to have the disasters happen to them—and those people would be uninsurable—and all the others wouldn't bother with it. But that's not my point; I wanted to question what would happen if the method was accurate, but too far outside the box for people to accept. If there wasn't an already recognized scientific discipline to pay attention to it, you'd find it hard to get people to buy into it.

"Scientists would dismiss it because it didn't fit their rules for how you find truth, religious people would reject it because they've already decided what Scripture means and are closed to anything of any significant difference, and atheists would dismiss it as too God-centered. So what would you do if you had this truth and felt compelled to get people to hear it?"

He didn't wait for an answer, but walked out, turned right, and opened the doors to the staircase that would take him down to the street. When the answer clicked in his head, Maurice jumped to the door and shouted down the stairs, but the older man had already left the building. Racing back into the classroom, he ran to the far wall, threw open the window, and spotted him down the block, in the exact middle of the street.

Afraid his words would be lost in the wind that had whipped up, he shouted as loud as he could, "Paul! Paul!"

The older man stopped, turned, looked up. Maurice shouted again, "Try fiction?"

Not loud enough; the older man shook his head, pointed to his ears, and yelled something Maurice couldn't hear either. He cupped his hands, leaned out farther, and tried again. "I said, would he try fiction?"

The words took a few seconds to reach their target, but when they did, Paul stood stock-still, as if a meteor had hit him. Then he walked back until he stood right under the window Maurice was leaning out of, and shouted up. "Sorry, did you say, 'try fiction'?"

Maurice nodded, and Paul continued, the words coming up as if out of a whirlwind. "Yes, sir, fiction, that's as good a place as any, I suppose. He might try fiction." He paused, turned to go, turned back for one last salvo. "But what if he didn't know how to write good fiction? How could he make sure the fiction mavens wouldn't also reject it, same as the scientists and religionists? Worse, what if fiction also wouldn't work?"

And he walked off. Still turning it over in his mind, Maurice went down the same stairs, found himself chasing after Paul, wanting to know more, too impatient to figure it out for himself. Which he would have, he always told himself, but hearing it was easier.

When he reached his new teacher, the white-haired man threw his coat over Maurice's shoulders, saying, "Here, it's getting cold, you don't want to catch your death." Maurice burrowed himself in its warmth, questions bubbling up in his throat.

As they walked in the exact middle of the road, up and down the street, the walls began to shake.